The Lost Hamsters of Barnaby Bunch

Michael Jude Schauer

ISBN 979-8-89043-115-8 (paperback)
ISBN 979-8-89043-116-5 (hardcover)
ISBN 979-8-89043-117-2 (digital)

Copyright © 2023 by Michael Jude Schauer

All rights reserved. No part of this publication may be reproduced, distributed, or transmitted in any form or by any means, including photocopying, recording, or other electronic or mechanical methods without the prior written permission of the publisher. For permission requests, solicit the publisher via the address below.

Christian Faith Publishing
832 Park Avenue
Meadville, PA 16335
www.christianfaithpublishing.com

Printed in the United States of America

To Dad.
Your chirp always made me laugh.
And to my grandchildren: Hazel, Isla, Calvin,
Audra, Joshua, Reese, Davis, and Aidan.
I pray that you will always choose the call of
the castle over the howl of the wolf.

Audible for The Lost Hamsters of Barnaby Bunch now available on Amazon, Apple, and Audible. Written by Michael Jude Schauer, read by Mo Egan, music by Phil Keaggy.

Contents

Part 1

Chapter 1: A Pirate's Funeral 1
Chapter 2: The Five Stones 8
Chapter 3: Je Vous Donne Mon Coeur 12
Chapter 4: Fort Chewy 16
Chapter 5: Silver Arrows 22
Chapter 6: A Berry Deep Sleep 27
Chapter 7: One Lost Hamster 32
Chapter 8: The Rapids 38
Chapter 9: Castello del Lupo 47
Chapter 10: Welcome to the Oubliette 51
Chapter 11: Rat Bite Fever 57
Chapter 12: Castle Secrets 62
Chapter 13: Night Songs 66
Chapter 14: Feather from the Sky 70
Chapter 15: The Wolf King 75
Chapter 16: Rats in the Walls 79
Chapter 17: Eau de Vie 86
Epilogue 93

Part 2

Chapter 18: Paffuto: The Five-Hundred-Pound Canary 97
Chapter 19: Spectacle of Light 101
Chapter 20: Angry Eyes 104
Chapter 21: Alzati Sopra 107
Chapter 22: In for a Penny, In for a Pound 112
Chapter 23: Beaks to the Grindstones 116
Chapter 24: Morte and Morendo 120
Chapter 25: Bite of the Vipers 123
Chapter 26: Cheese in the Trap 127
Chapter 27: Sticky Cats 132
Chapter 28: Wolf Moon 135
Chapter 29: To Snort Another Day 138
Chapter 30: Twister of Words 142
Chapter 31: The Glastonbury Thorn 147
Chapter 32: Sky Watchers 151
Chapter 33: The Bite of the Trap 155
Chapter 34: No Whistle, No Chirp 158
Chapter 35: Archers, Loose! 161
Chapter 36: Pardon et Repos 168
Chapter 37: Coeur des Coeurs 173
Epilogue 181

Notes for Part 1 and Part 2 183

The Lost Hamsters of Barnaby Bunch

Part 1

Chapter 1

A Pirate's Funeral

His hands were cold and stiff as he fumbled with the key to unlock the door. On a frosty dark morning, the hanging sign squeaked back and forth above his head in the biting wind. The sign read, "Stumpy's Pet Shop." He could see puffs of his own misty breath as he exhaled. His fogged glasses and the morning darkness made it difficult to unlock the door that separated himself from the hungry animals waiting inside. Barnaby Bunch was a tall and slender man, slightly hunched at the shoulders from age. His deep-blue eyes were kind and inviting. He never withheld compassion from any man or beast. Barnaby's responsibility was to open Stumpy's Pet Shop at four o'clock each morning. His job was to clean cages and feed hundreds of hungry animals. Even though he didn't own the pet store, Barnaby poured his heart and soul into the tender care of each animal. He treated them as if they were his own. If a capuchin monkey had a stubborn bellyache, Barnaby would take the little fellow home at night to pamper him back to health. When a parrot seemed lonely or downhearted, Barnaby would stay overnight at the shop and sing soft Irish lullabies until her spirits lifted, helping her drift back to sleep on her java perch.

Stumpy's Pet Shop was named after the owner, Gustavo Stump, who sadly was no longer alive. Gustavo met a tragic and horrific death while doing what he loved the most, searching the world for exotic animals. Poor Gustavo was on an expedition to discover new parrot species in the Borneo River Basin, when he was devoured by a goliath Yateveo plant, the largest carnivorous plant in the world. Later, a local tribesman said that there was nothing left of poor Gustavo Stump except his leather hiking boots, which the Yateveo spit out while trying to digest the explorer.

At the reading of Gustavo's last will and testament, Gustavo's son, Ichabod, broke down in tears. Everyone thought that he was crying because of the tragic loss of his father. But no, he was crying because he found out that his father had left him the pet shop, which he hated with a passion. You see, Ichabod was not like his father at all. He hated animals. He thought all animals were foul, coarse, and altogether disgusting. The pet shop *should* have been left to Barnaby, who adored animals, but it was left to the next of kin instead. And the next of kin was Ichabod, his son.

Later, when Ichabod found out that he could make a fortune *selling* his father's exotic animals, he accepted his inheritance, but only on one condition. He wanted Barnaby to continue working at the pet shop to take care of the animals so *he* wouldn't have to. He didn't particularly like Barnaby; but Barnaby knew how to feed, care for, and love all the animals in the pet shop. This made him very valuable to Ichabod. When Barnaby was caring for the animals, it made his heart sing with joy. When Ichabod even looked at the animals, he became light-headed and queasy, especially when he smelled or even looked at monkey poo. Life isn't always fair. Sometimes wonderful, animal-loving people get swallowed by man-eating plants. And sometimes selfish, disgusting people inherit pet shops even though they couldn't care less if animals ever existed at all.

Ichabod Percival Stump was a grotesque and repulsive little man. He was an extremely unpleasant character with a contrary disposition and vulgar manners. His body was extremely offensive, not because he was short of stature and as round as a melon, but because he never felt the need to bathe. He had the unsavory odor of an overripe squash that had aged in the sun. Ichabod also reeked of cigar smoke, but when it intermingled with the odious smell of aged cabbage and Camembert cheese, which he nibbled incessantly, it created an invisible cloud that hovered over him wherever he went. He sported an untrimmed mustache that hung over his upper lip and fluttered when he breathed heavily with his open mouth. And when his wheezing mouth hung open, his teeth were revealed, which were the color of field corn and highly disorganized, like a picket fence after a tornado.

Ichabod Stump probably grew to hate animals because he feared them. As a very young lad, Ichabod Percival Stump was walking home from school on a cool fall day when a baby squirrel accidentally fell out of a tree. While Ichabod was walking on a path below, the frightened squirrel fell from a branch and landed right on his shoulder. The scared animal dug his claws into his sweater and hung on with all his might. Ichabod ran home, screaming in terror! He was sure that he was going to be eaten alive by the *tree monster*. When he reached the safety of his home, his father, Gustavo, heard his son screaming and ran out to find the cause of his mental torment. The elder Stump simply cupped the tiny squirrel in his soft big hands and gently shushed the little fellow, until he relaxed and let go of Ichabod's woolen sweater. He placed the frightened squirrel on the branch of a nearby maple tree, not paying too much attention to his son's agitation. But on that day, a seed of fear was planted deep in Ichabod's heart, and he feared *all* animals from that moment on. Fear often leads to hate, and Ichabod P. Stump hated all animals from that day forward, especially squirrels. He grew up believing that all squirrels were plotting to kill him.

Barnaby Bunch finally heard the click of cold metal as the key turned in the lock. Grabbing the door handle to the pet shop, he pushed it open. He entered the warm shop, trying to peer through his fogged glasses. He was greeted by the erupting clatter of unfed beasts. Barnaby extended his arms upward with outstretched hands. Then he shouted, as he did every morning, "Good morning, lads and lassies!" Barnaby knew that there would be an even louder explosion of squawking, chirping, chattering, whooping, and screeching. Breakfast time in a pet shop is quite an uproarious event. Barnaby looked lovingly around the shop. There were beautiful parrots of every kind. There were African grays, rainbow lorikeets, blue-throated macaws, rosy-faced lovebirds, and, of course, three gorgeous cockatiels who were also very close sisters. There were jabbering monkeys as well. He cared for squirrel, spider, and finger monkeys, which are more accurately called pygmy marmosets. He also cared for golden lion tamarins and three delightful capuchins, who were also very close brothers. There were many other animals in his care as well. There were rabbits galore and lizards of various sizes and temperaments. There were Mongolian and fat-tailed gerbils, hedgehogs, ringtail lemurs, and African clawless otters. The snakes in the pet shop were nonvenomous with wonderful personalities. There were rosy boas, milk snakes and green corn snakes. The pet shop even had Silkie chickens in every color. The bearded blue Silkies were Barnaby's favorite. If you looked up Silkie chickens in Smithson's *World Book of Poultry*, you would find that they are the most majestic of all chickens and quite attractive. However, all the animals in Stumpy's Pet Shop were very special in their own way.

Barnaby had been working feverishly to clean messy cages and feeding *his children*, so he didn't hear the shop door open at first. Once he caught a nauseating whiff of stale cigar smoke, he knew who had entered the pet shop. It was Ichabod Percival Stump, his crabby and crotchety boss.

"Barnaby Bunch! Where are you?" Ichabod sounded gruff and short tempered.

"Here, sir, by the monkey cages." Barnaby stood up and raised a hand with a quick wave. Ichabod waddled back to where Barnaby had been cleaning out a squirrel monkey cage. As Ichabod approached, he gagged and shuddered from the smell.

"Shouldn't you be done by now, Bunch?" He held his scarf close to his nose. "I'm not paying you to play with the monkeys! Maybe you should start coming in earlier," Ichabod said in an irritated tone. As he looked up at the much taller Barnaby, he blew cigar smoke up into his face and watched as Barnaby held back a cough. After the smoke cleared, Ichabod Stump continued to look up at Barnaby, then cleared his throat to speak.

"Bunch, *we* have a problem," said Ichabod.

"We do, sir?" Barnaby asked quietly.

"Yes, *we* do!" Ichabod fired back. "Have you seen the hamster pen, Bunch? They are out of control!"

"Out of...control, sir?" Barnaby asked in a confused manner.

"Yes, man! Out of control!" he said with a raised voice. "At the beginning of the month, we had fifteen hamsters in stock. Do you know how many we have now? Well, do you?" shouted Ichabod.

"N...n...not exactly, Mr. Stump, sir." Barnaby had a feeling he was about to find out.

"Sixty-two! We have sixty-two of those miserable circus rats! They are multiplying out of control, and no one is buying them. And yet we still have to feed them. That is costing *me* money. That is *our* problem!"

"I'm not sure what you would have me do, sir," a confused Barnaby replied.

Ichabod Stump turned away from Barnaby without uttering another word. He tottered down the store aisle, then turned left and walked through an opening into the *slop room*. This room held a large stone stationary tub with a leaky old faucet. Ichabod turned on the tap and began filling the old stone sink that was used to clean feeding bowls and drinking tubes. Ichabod reappeared and slowly walked up to Barnaby. He left the water running, filling up the large stone tub.

"There is only one obvious solution, Bunch," Ichabod said without blinking. Barnaby suddenly realized that Ichabod wanted him to give the hamsters a pirate's funeral. Ichabod wanted the hamsters to be dropped into the tub water since they were *in the way* and *out of control,* but Barnaby knew they couldn't swim.

"No, Mr. Stump! I will never do that! I couldn't!" Barnaby was visibly shaken at the very thought of ending these beautiful tiny creatures.

"You can and you will, Bunch! If you don't, you will no longer work in my pet shop!" Ichabod warned. "Introduce your little friends to their watery grave by the end of the day. Now go and shut off the faucet or you'll be paying the water bill out of your next paycheck!" And with that, Ichabod Stump turned and hobble-waddled slowly out of the store. Barnaby stood in front of the hamster pen, looking down at sixty-two sad furry faces. It was almost as if they heard and understood what Ichabod wanted Barnaby to do. They were huddled close together and shaking with fright. Barnaby looked in their eyes and could see their fear, when suddenly he heard water splashing on the tile floor in the slop room. He was jolted back into focus and ran to the slop room and quickly turned off the tap. The tub was filled to the brim with icy water splashing on his shoes. After he shut the water off, Barnaby looked in the tub for a moment to see his own reflection in the water. It felt like he was looking deep into his own soul. He walked slowly back to the hamster pen not knowing what he was going to do. He looked once again into the tiny dotty black eyes of the helpless creatures. There were a few moments of silence when he unexpectedly heard a shaky small voice emerge from the pen.

"We…we…can't swim!" whimpered a timid voice from the pen. Barnaby thought he was hearing with his emotions and not his ears. He then heard another squeaky voice from the pen.

"We'll sink like rocks!" squealed another voice. Barnaby was beside himself with excitement.

"You can talk!" he shouted.

"Of course we can talk! Do we look like simpletons?" shouted a very annoyed and offended voice from the crowd of hamsters.

"No, no, I just didn't think you were as smart as other animals, like dolphins," said Barnaby.

"Dolphins? Don't insult us!" cried the indignant hamster. "Dolphins are just big, dumb fish!"

Another hamster that had more experience in the sciences, and especially marine biology, felt the need to correct the indignant hamster's understanding of a dolphin's classification in the animal kingdom. "Mammalia. Dolphins are mammals. You said fish, but dolphins are mammals, just like us," answered the more educated hamster. "They are warm-blooded cetaceans. They breathe air and suckle their young."

"Excuuuse me, Professor. They are absolutely nothing like us," the indignant hamster replied.

Barnaby was dumbstruck. He could only listen to the two hamsters with a dropped jaw and mouth wide open as they continued to chatter about marine life. Barnaby could not believe what he was hearing. He didn't care *what* they were talking about, just that they were *talking*! He was listening to *talking hamsters*!

A small, and very shy, hamster timidly spoke up. "You wouldn't really…finish us, would you?" asked the hamster.

"Of course I wouldn't. I couldn't!" replied Barnaby. "But I don't know what to do!"

He sank to the floor and started to think, *How can I save the job I love* and *these precious creatures*? His heart was torn.

Chapter 2

The Five Stones

Barnaby sat on the cold floor beneath the hamster pen, listening to the squeaks and chirps of sixty-two terrified souls. He pulled his collar up and slipped both hands into his pockets to keep warm. In one pocket, he felt the small leather book that his grandfather had given to him so long ago. He still carried it to feel close to the man who raised him with boundless love and compassion. He pulled the book out of his pocket and looked at the cover, which read, "Songs of Light." He felt comforted just holding it in his hands. He slowly opened the book to a page that had been marked by his grandfather long ago. Barnaby began to read its words in a whisper:

> In the middle of the darkest night
> When dreams away have flown,
> Souls in anguish slowly die
> And wither all alone.
>
> Amid a growing, bleak despair
> A distant spark will glow,
> The flame of life begins to burn
> And hope is soon to grow.

The words burned hot in his soul. He stood up quickly and peered inside the hamster pen. Their tiny faces looked back at him in fear. They had just been sentenced to death. Was this *their darkest night*, spoken of in the song? Their *souls* did seem to be *in anguish*. Were the lines from the *Songs of Light* talking about these lost and utterly defenseless hamsters? Then Barnaby thought, *Maybe I am the spark that is beginning to glow amid their growing, bleak despair. Maybe I am to be their hope.* He quickly turned the page and read on excitedly:

> Stones of power
> Stones of light
> Stones to guide you
> Through the night
>
> Stones to deliver
> Stones to save
> Stones for the humble
> And stones for the brave
>
> Stones to calm rivers
> Stones to ease fears
> Stones to move mountains
> And stones to dry tears
>
> Stones for the lowly
> Stones for the weak
> Stones for the gentle
> And stones for the meek

    Barnaby grew even more excited as he devoured the words. The songs about stones struck his heart like a thunderbolt, and the words seemed to leap right off the page. He rose from where he was slumped under the hamster pen and looked down at the sad, shivering creatures. He quickly moved toward a supply room down the hall. After entering the cluttered room, he pulled a stool up to a leaning metal shelf. He reached to the top and fumbled for an old tin box with a bent rusty lid. He pulled it down as the stool wobbled slightly.

After sitting down on the stool, he placed the tin box on his lap. He paused, then took a deep breath. He looked down and read the top of the lid, "Bivosky's Breakfast Cocoa." He pried the dusty lid off slowly with his fingertips. With the box opened, he looked down inside and saw a worn leather pouch with a tattered drawstring. He opened the pouch slowly and poured five colored stones into his hand. He trembled as a thought came to him like a sudden gust of wind. *Could these be the same five stones spoken of in the* Songs of Light?

As he held the stones in his quivering hands, he thought back to a story that Gustavo Stump had told him before he met his fateful end. Gustavo brought the five stones back from an expedition. Exploring the Yasuni Rainforest in Ecuador, Gustavo was searching for finger monkeys. He came upon a man who was also searching for these elusive creatures. Ecuadorian finger monkeys are extremely rare and unique because they can speak, like parrots. But they don't just imitate language patterns like parrots. Their speech is a fully developed, intelligent expression of thoughts and words. A mature finger monkey can hold conversations ranging from Roman history to modern architecture. Both Gustavo and the stranger had been searching for these unusual, magnificent creatures. Their paths crossed when Gustavo had just discovered three healthy finger monkeys and was ready to return home to his pet shop. The man that he encountered was an archeologist who had recently discovered the five stones while on another expedition to dig up the Pilgrim Road in Jerusalem. The man was willing to trade the five stones he unearthed because he thought he could make a greater fortune with a talking finger monkey. Gustavo had read about the stones in the *Songs of Light* and believed in their power. So under the shade of a giant kapok tree, the two men agreed to trade one talking pygmy marmoset, or finger monkey, for five pilgrim stones. Only three toucans, four tree frogs, and a snake witnessed the transaction from the branches of the great tree. The archeologist went his way with a single talking finger monkey, and Gustavo went in the opposite direction with his other two finger monkeys and a pouch of five stones that could change the world.

THE LOST HAMSTERS OF BARNABY BUNCH

The misguided archeologist was blinded by greed and selfish desire. Presenting a tiny talking monkey in a circus or maybe a sideshow would make him rich and famous, or so he thought. The archeologist was not a kind man, so Franklin the Fabulous Finger Monkey, as he was billed, refused to speak for paying customers, and soon the greedy archeologist went out of business. He subsequently chased Franklin away in a fit of rage. Franklin, who was skilled in cartography and demography geography, easily found his way back to Gustavo and was reunited with his finger monkey siblings.

When Gustavo returned to the pet shop, he only shared the story of the five stones with Barnaby. He showed Barnaby where the stones would be kept. He wanted someone to know where the stones were hidden in case he met an untimely death. He told Barnaby that according to the *Songs of Light*, the stones were to be given to the lowly, the weak, the gentle, and the meek. Barnaby meditated on Gustavo's instructions as he turned over each stone in his hand. He gasped when he saw words etched on each of the stones. As he read each word, the fire in his heart grew, confirming to him that these were the *true stones* discovered under the Pilgrim Road.

Gustavo didn't reveal his knowledge of the stones to his own son, Ichabod, because he knew that Ichabod would never understand their true value or purpose. He would most likely sell them for selfish gain. But Gustavo knew that Barnaby's heart was pure and faithful and that he would be a trustworthy keeper of the stones. And now Barnaby held the five stones in his own trembling hands, believing that they were to be given to the hamsters who were just given a death sentence. He had never known anyone more meek, gentle, weak, or lowly than these beautiful furry creatures. Barnaby knew in his heart what had to be done. He raced back to the hamster enclosure and stood before the sixty-two trembling souls, holding the stones tightly in his fist.

Chapter 3

Je Vous Donne Mon Coeur

As Barnaby looked down at the frightened furry faces of the tiny hamsters, he knew in his heart that he couldn't let them suffer in a slop tub filled with icy water. He believed they were being called for a higher purpose. But he also knew that the hamster pen had to be empty when Ichabod returned. Barnaby continued to look at the sad faces of sixty-two souls who were awaiting their fate.

"I am truly lost," Barnaby said to the shivering hamsters, "and if I feel lost, you must feel lost as well. You beautiful, lost creatures. You wonderful, lost hamsters."

After a few moments, Barnaby heard his own words. "Lost hamsters? That's it!" cried Barnaby. "Brilliant! You *are* the lost hamsters! I must make you *lost*!"

Barnaby raced back to the storeroom and quickly pulled down a large wicker basket from a tall metal shelf. He folded a paint-stained old tarp to line the bottom of the basket. Grabbing the two handles on the basket's ends, he turned it to fit through the doorway before carrying it back to the hamster pen. He placed it on the floor in front of the pen, then looked back into the faces of the waiting hamsters. The biggest and oldest hamster in the pen maneuvered himself through a maze of tiny furry bodies to speak. Barnaby wondered if he was their leader and spokesman.

"Might you have a name, large hamster?" Barnaby spoke to him directly.

"I do, sir. My name is Captain Nathaniel Nibbles. I am the oldest and most respected hamster in this lot." He spoke with authority.

"Do you *all* have names?" asked Barnaby.

"We do, sir. Every hamster is celebrated with a name on the day of their glorious birth into this world." He looked around at the hamsters closest to him and began to introduce them to Barnaby. "This is Chadwick the Holy, and next to him is Cletus. And next to Cletus and down the line there's Einstein, Two-Spots, and Giggles." Just as Captain Nibbles introduced Giggles, Giggles did just that. He began to giggle. "Then there's Cheerio, who has never had a dark cloud pass over him. His world is sunshine and rainbows. Next is Skittles, followed by Puff Bottom. And then you have Wendell Cheeks, Mr. Whiskers, Sassypants, Freckles, Biscuit, and the sisters, Lola and Rosie." Captain Nibbles would have kept going, but Barnaby stopped him.

"Maybe you can introduce me to the rest later, but I fear that trying to remember the names of sixty-two hamsters on this stressful night would be a tricky proposition for me." Barnaby paused, then continued, "Captain Nibbles, do you trust me?"

"Sir, you have us at a disadvantage. We have no choice. There is no one else to trust," Captain Nibbles said with an honest heart.

"I have a plan to help you all, but *we must hurry*," warned Barnaby. "First, you all need to get in this basket, then we are going on a journey. I must lead you all from this dreadful place." The hamsters all squeak-cheered when they heard his words.

"We don't need much motivation, sir! Fear is a fine spur. Our very lives are in your kind hands." Captain Nibbles spoke for all the hamsters. Barnaby began to place each of the hamsters into the waiting basket, starting with Captain Nibbles. He then started picking them up two at a time. Chadwick the Holy and Cletus were next to be lowered in the basket. Then came Einstein and Two-Spots followed by Giggles and Cheerio. Cheerio couldn't stop smiling, and Giggles couldn't stop giggling. Each hamster wanted to introduce themselves to Barnaby as he picked them up to place them gently in the basket. He was pleased to meet Buffy and Buttercup, followed by Corky and Eye Patch. He greeted Chewy and Houdini, then the twins, Cheese and Crackers. Jiggety Jumper, a very excitable hamster, was hard to handle as he almost jumped out of Barnaby's hand. Barnaby had to use two hands to hold on to Jiggety. The next hamster to be picked up by Barnaby was an unusual little fellow named Julian Boucharde. Julian was a French hamster who made his way across the ocean by stowing away on a cargo ship. He was full of life and always ready for an adventure.

"Je vous donne mon coeur, Maître Bunch," said Julian Boucharde with all sincerity. Barnaby knew very little French, but he thought he understood that Julian was saying something like "My heart belongs to you." Soon, all sixty-two hamsters were packed safely and snuggly into the basket. They looked like one giant ball of fur all smushed together. Barnaby picked the basket up by its handles and moved toward the entrance of the pet shop. He turned to the other animals before leaving the pet shop and felt the need to give them last-minute instructions.

"Goodbye, me wee lads and lassies. I'll be back soon. Garden lizards, you'll be eatin' all your crickets, now. Parrots, no coarse words are to be spurtin' from your beaks. And monkeys, no tossin' yer poo! Now, all of yas, behave while I'm gone." Barnaby was talking to one baby howler monkey in particular, but he didn't want to call out his name for fear that it would embarrass him.

Barnaby Bunch walked out of the pet shop clutching the hamster basket tightly. His heart was filled with peace as soon as he chose to perform such an honorable and noble deed. As he walked toward his rusty old pickup truck, the basket bounced in his hands, and he could hear giggling coming from inside the basket. He loaded the basket into the back of his truck, then he climbed into the driver's seat. It took a few tries to start the engine. The truck sputtered and choked before it finally started. The hamsters in the back were huddled together, feeling the cool air ruffling their soft fur. Most of the hamsters had never been outside of the pet shop before, so their hearts were beating wildly with anticipation. As the truck drove down the road, the hamsters wondered where they were going. They only knew one thing: Barnaby was their only hope, and their trust was firmly placed in him.

Barnaby continued to drive, occasionally looking over his shoulder through the back window to make sure none of the hamsters had bounced out of the basket. He drove for over an hour deep into the countryside. He drove up hills and down hills and over three bridges that spanned three wide rivers. He slowed down to find an exit from the main road. After turning down a narrow dirt road, he drove until a forest began to emerge. The dirt road was pitted and choppy. At one point, Barnaby looked back into the bed of his truck and saw the basket lift into the air, then crash back down. He heard loud giggling and comments like "Wheeee!" and "Do it again!" and "Get your stinkin' foot out of my ear!"

Barnaby continued to drive deeper into the backwoods, farther and farther from civilization. The canopy of the broad-leaved trees began to block out the remaining sunlight, and Barnaby knew that he was now far from the dangers of Ichabod's cold, unfeeling heart. It was hardly even a road anymore, and Barnaby finally felt that it was safe to pull his truck to a stop. He turned off the engine, climbed out of the driver's seat, walked to the back of the truck, then lowered the tailgate. He reached out and took one of the handles of the basket and pulled it toward himself. He looked down into the pile of fur and smiled.

"You are all safe now. No one's going to hurt you," Barnaby said with a soft comfort in his voice as he looked lovingly into the basket. He saw Buffy's eyes fill with tears. He knew these were tears of gratitude. Then Sassypants popped his head up and ruined the tender moment with a bit of saucy rudeness.

"If we can survive your horrible driving, we can survive anything," he said without a single thought of being thankful.

"We have learned to ignore Sassypants," said Captain Nibbles. "His nickname is the Fish. Just like a fish, his lips are always moving; but nothing important comes out, only air bubbles." Captain Nibbles then grew very serious and paused before speaking.

"What is next, Master Barnaby?" asked the captain.

Barnaby looked into his eyes, patted him on his tiny head, and said, "It is time to be extraordinarily brave, my little friend."

Chapter 4

Fort Chewy

Barnaby Bunch knew that it was time to say goodbye when his heart began to ache. Saying goodbye to someone that you care about always causes a deep sadness that can overwhelm you. He looked deeply into the eyes of each helpless tiny hamster as he wished them all of heaven's blessings. He was not only sad when he said goodbye but was also frightened for them since he knew the dangers that awaited them in the shadowy forest. Barnaby knew about the wily fox, the shifty weasel, and the ill-tempered bobcats. But he also knew about the wild pigs with gnarly, gnashing tusks hiding in the brush. There were even rumors that a very large cinnamon bear was wandering the forest. But by far, the biggest fear that haunted him was the castle full of wolves. They knew how to paralyze every animal in the forest with fear. The castle wolves ruled over all with their wicked hearts and deceitful schemes. Barnaby lowered the basket slowly to the ground, then, ever so gently, tipped it on its side. The hamsters tumbled softly to the ground into one big cluster of fur.

"This forest is your new home, my wee furry friends. Remember, you've got to do yer own growin' no matter how tall your father was," Barnaby shared as the last hamster rolled out of the tipped basket. "You must all stick together and listen closely to your Captain Nibbles. Your survival depends on trusting him."

"You won't leave us, will you, Master Bunch?" asked Cheerio.

"I'll be leavin' you in one way, but stay'n in another. Our paths will be crossin' again, I promise you that. I must go back now to care for the other animals in the pet shop. They need me," said Barnaby. "I have a capuchin who still has frightfully bad manners and a red-bellied lemur who still won't touch his fruit."

"This is our life now," declared Captain Nibbles. "We will not only survive—we will flourish! We will always remember you and honor you, Master Barnaby. You showed us more than a kindness: you saved our lives. Now we have hope." There were many hamster tears, and everyone found it difficult to say goodbye. Barnaby called Captain Nibbles away from the others so he could speak privately.

"Take these," Barnaby said as he pressed a small leather pouch into Captain Nibbles's tiny hands and against his furry chest. "There are five extraordinary stones within this pouch," Barnaby continued. "They will be a great help when you need them the most. But these stones are much more than stones. They have the power to change the world. Hold them close to your heart and never doubt their power."

"I'm sorry, I don't understand, Master Barnaby," the captain said in confusion.

"My mind is a little jumble-muddled too, but I believe in my heart that Gustavo was speaking about you, Captain Nibbles," answered Barnaby. "*You* are favored to receive the five stones, and *you* are chosen to lead an army."

Captain Nibbles looked over at the sad group of misfit hamsters. Two-Spots was lying on his back and sucking in air to see how high he could make his belly rise, and Buttercup was on all fours, making hissing sounds like a cat to make his friends laugh.

"And *that* is the army that I am supposed to lead?" he asked warily.

"Don't look at them with your eyes. See them with your heart," answered Barnaby. "You were born to lead, Captain Nibbles. Anyone can hold the wheel when the sea is peaceful. You were destined to guide the wheel through the coming storm."

"So *now* I'm leading an army *and* guiding a ship through a storm? How do you know if the stones even work? How do you know if they are special at all?" asked Captain Nibbles with doubt in his voice. Barnaby took the small leather-bound book out of another inside pocket. The book had the words *Songs of Light* burnished on the cover.

"This book," whispered Barnaby, "speaks of the five stones. A different word is revealed on each stone. The five words are *flame, life, hope, light,* and *water.*" Barnaby handed the book to the captain. "Keep this book close to your heart. Devour every page and let every word burn inside you," Barnaby said earnestly.

"How will I know when to use them?" asked Captain Nibbles.

"You will know," Barnaby answered. "I know that you have been chosen for a greater purpose." Captain Nibbles tucked the pouch with the stones inside his leather vest. He and Barnaby then turned back to the other hamsters. Their somber conversation was interrupted by Chewy, who was very excited to ask Barnaby a very important question.

"Mr. Barnaby, sir, may we…keep the basket? I think we could use it to make an outstanding fort. We could turn it upside down, chew a door in the side, and use it as a headquarters or something," said Chewy with confidence.

"Of course, you may keep it, laddie," answered Barnaby. "And I know it will be a very fine fort, as long as you build it for the others and not just yourself. Now, I better be getting back to the pet shop. I'll have to convince Ichabod that his hamster problem is solved. We all have a big secret to keep. Till we meet again!" Barnaby offered them a wink and a broad smile. He climbed back into his truck, started it, and began the long drive back to the pet shop. As Barnaby drove away, Captain Nibbles ordered all hamsters on deck to grab an edge of the basket. Sixty-two hamsters strong dragged the basket from the side of the road into the trees and disappeared into the thickness of the forest. They carried the basket along a deer path for over a hundred feet until they came to a clearing. Captain Nibbles ordered them to stop and lower the basket to the ground. There it sat, upside down, under a tall white oak tree. A splendid fairy wren watched curiously from one of its thick branches. The exhausted hamsters collapsed after setting the basket down. Still breathing hard, Chewy pushed his way forward, insisting on using his special skills to help.

"Captain Nibbles, sir!" Chewy saluted as if he was in the military.

"There's no need to salute, Chewy. What is on your mind?" Captain Nibbles replied.

"I would like to prepare the fort, sir," Chewy answered.

"Prepare the fort?" questioned the captain.

"Sir, we need an entrance to our fort, and I believe I'm the right hamster for the job. There is a reason they call me Chewy, sir. Look at these choppers, sir," Chewy said as he opened his mouth to proudly show off his impressive biters.

"Yes, a remarkable set of ivories, indeed! So you want to chew through the basket to make an entrance to our fort?" Captain Nibbles inquired.

"Yes, sir, immediately, sir," Chewy said with confidence.

"You are a bag full of brains and a bushel full of heart, Chewy," proclaimed Captain Nibbles. "Mr. Whiskers and Einstein, please join Chewy and commence chewing! Prepare the fort!"

Mr. Whiskers was an extremely gifted architect with clever artistic skills. Einstein had remarkable mathematical abilities, and his expertise in calculations was unmatched. The two of them would be a great asset in helping Chewy design and construct a safe and strong entryway into the new fort.

Before the sun set, Chewy and his friends created a magnificent entrance to their brand-new headquarters. It was very impressive for a band of lost hamsters. They chewed away a perfect door that they could reattach by making hinges using strips of material from the tarp that had lined their getaway basket. They now had a door that could open and close, with an intricate locking system, offering protection from ravenous carnivores at night. It was an incredibly designed door that won Chewy, Mr. Whiskers, and Einstein the admiration and praise from all the hamsters, including Captain Nibbles. In fact, Captain Nibbles was so impressed that he declared that the fort should be named Fort Chewy, in honor of Chewy, who took such a great interest in keeping all the hamsters safe and secure.

The tangerine glow of the setting sun seemed to melt over the mountains behind them. A damp chill of the evening air started to settle on them when Captain Nibbles called the hamsters together.

"Tomorrow we'll explore the forest for food and water, but tonight we'll enter Fort Chewy, huddle to stay warm, and get a good night's rest. This has been a very frightening and unsettling day. Today we came very close to meeting our sad end in an icy slop tub. In the end, we are just a group of lost hamsters on the run, scampering about the unknown; but let us always remember the man who stood in the gap for us and valued us more than diamonds, Barnaby Bunch!"

After Captain Nibbles had spoken, there was an abundance of cheers and rivers of tears as they could still feel the fear that gripped them earlier that day in the pet shop. They believed in their hearts that they had been rescued for a higher purpose, and they were all being called to be extraordinary.

As the hamsters stood in silence remembering the goodness and mercy of Barnaby Bunch, the stillness of the moment was suddenly interrupted by a piercing, heart-stopping sound. The hamsters could hear, off in the distance, the distinct and unmistakable howl…of wolves.

"To the fort!" Captain Nibbles commanded. And with one single command, sixty-one hamsters scampered quickly into the safety of Fort Chewy. After every hamster was safely gathered inside the fort, Captain Nibbles backed in slowly through the open door staring out into the darkness. After he had entered, he could hear Chewy and Einstein on either side of the door shouting.

"Secure the gate!" they cried in unison. They quickly closed and latched the door with all sixty-two hamsters tucked safely inside. After the hamsters had stopped shaking and were all settled for the night, Captain Nibbles took out the *Songs of Light* that Barnaby had given him. The captain began to read the marked pages of the tiny leather book. His heart began to beat faster as he read the words by the glowing light of the full moon:

> Amid the growing, bleak despair
> A distant spark will glow,
> The flame of life begins to burn,
> And hope is soon to grow.

THE LOST HAMSTERS OF BARNABY BUNCH

He devoured the next page like a bowl full of fresh sunflower seeds:

> Stones of power
> Stones of light
> Stones to guide you
> Through the night

After he read the words *lowly*, *weak*, *gentle*, and *meek*, he looked over at the other sixty-one hamsters who were gently falling asleep. A flame ignited deep inside him as he realized that these *lost hamsters* before him were being described by the divine words he was reading. He began to understand what Master Barnaby was trying to tell him. After reading the description of the stones, over and over, Captain Nibbles closed the book and held it close to his chest. He looked up at the full moon and whispered into the cold night air, "I am ready, sir. I will take the wheel in the storm."

Chapter 5

Silver Arrows

Captain Nibbles set out to find food and water for sixty-two hamsters. They also needed bows and arrows to protect themselves from aggressive and vicious carnivores. So the captain assembled a small band of hamster explorers to set out on a mission to find all the supplies they needed. He chose Chewy, Two-Spots, and Corky to be trained as his most trusted archers. He also chose Biscuit and Cletus because they were brilliant translators; and they could both speak fox, beaver, and even bear in case of emergency. Biscuit was even proficient in speaking porcupine if one should happen to cross their path. They left at dawn, leaving Chadwick the Holy in charge of those left behind at Fort Chewy.

They found food first. Summer-crisp pear trees flourished in a small grove, and the gatherers took as many of the juicy pears as they could fit into the wattled baskets that they were toting. They also filled their rucksacks with okra seeds, blackberries, and button mushrooms. The hamsters in the fort would be delighted with such a fine assortment, especially after days of having nothing to eat at all. The archers found very sturdy ironwood sticks to make the shafts for arrows but still could not find a suitable material for arrow tips. They were just about ready to give up and head back to Fort Chewy when Captain Nibbles noticed a column of smoke rising above a cluster of treetops.

It looked as if the rising smoke was extremely close by, so the small company of explorers decided to investigate. As they cautiously pushed their way through the old-growth forest, they found a wall of very dense blackthorn shrubs and wild myrtle bushes. They peered through the thickets to see a company of hardworking and very focused badgers. The leader of this badger colony was wearing a heavy leather apron, bending over a huge cast-iron pot. The pot was hovering over a hot open flame, and he was stirring the contents with a heavy black iron ladle. Two-Spots was hoping that it was purple potato soup, probably because he was starving, but Captain Nibbles told him that the badger was a silversmith and that he was smelting silver. The hamsters carefully maneuvered through the brambles to greet the badger.

"Greetings, kind sir!" Captain Nibbles said in a pleasant, reassuring voice.

"Good day, wee travelers!" Badger replied. "What brings you this deep into our humble neck of the forest?"

"We have other hamster friends who are relying on us to bring back food and water. But we also need materials for arms to protect our lot," answered the captain.

"Aye, you can't be too careful in this dark forest. Dangers lurk around every tree," said Badger. "What materials are you seeking?"

"Arrow tips, sir. Do your skills include fashioning silver tips for needle arrows?" Captain Nibbles questioned.

"You are blessed with favor and luck today. It is one of my specialities to be sure," boasted Badger as he stood up and straightened himself. Do you have the shafts in your possession?"

"We do. Fashioned out of ironwood, they are. We only have need of the tips, and we'd be blessed beyond measure if a fletcher could add the feathered flights," Captain Nibbles answered.

"Ahhh, yes. A good arrow needs handsome and hearty feathers to help guide it to its desired destination," Badger replied. "It just so happens that a fletcher travels through these parts from time to time and supplies me with the flights for the arrows I make. He borrows the feathers from quetzals, a beautiful bird with breathtaking tail feathers. They are not only brightly colored, but very sturdy to guide an arrow."

Captain Nibbles was excited to initiate a trade. "I would gladly trade two, no, three baskets of luscious, juice-drippy pears for, let's say, thirty silver arrow tips and thirty quetzal flights," bargained Captain Nibbles. He just knew how much badgers loved juicy, sloppy fruit.

"Hmmm…I *would* require a slurpy sample first," said Badger.

"Corky, bring the kind sir a taste of heaven's sweet nectar," the captain ordered.

He was confident that Badger would love the invigorating pear and would be more than willing to make a deal. After taking a big juicy bite, Badger slurped another bite, then another. After that, he said he needed just one more pear to be sure.

"Make it four baskets and I'll throw in nine silver daggers and a strapping bobbin of fishing line. You never know when that'll come in to play. Do we have a deal, little traveler?" Badger inquired, confident that he was getting the better side of the deal.

Captain Nibbles knew that with extra effort, they could easily replace the pears in their baskets from an abundant supply in the pear tree grove. They could stop and gather more on their way back to satisfy the waiting hamsters.

"You drive a hard bargain, sir, but a deal it is," said the captain.

Badger started to fill arrowhead molds with melted liquid silver as the hamsters drew closer to watch the silversmith work.

"Badger, sir, how do you know when the silver is refined enough for full strength and perfection?" Corky inquired.

"Look into the melted silver, young hamster, and tell me what you see," answered Badger. Corky looked over the edge of the pot, into the hot liquid silver.

"It's my face! It's my reflection! Fancy that, a silver-faced Corky!" cried Corky.

"That means the silver is ready, young hamster. I have been skimming the dross and every blemish from the surface for hours. All the impurities rise to the top, then I skim them off. When there are no more impurities and you can see your reflection, well, there you have it—the silver is perfected," Badger patiently explained.

"Ahhh, yes, reflection perfection," Corky replied. Corky noticed that there was a young badger on the other side of the pot who was also staring into the melted silver. She seemed mesmerized by her own image and frozen in a single position.

"What is the malady that this young badger suffers from, sir?" asked Corky delicately.

"Oh, her name is Narcy. It's a very heart-weepy tale, indeed. If you stare at your own image for *too* long, you become fixed on nothing other than your own appearance. She has become useless to the service of the other badgers or anyone else in the forest. She sits for days upon end, staring at her own reflection. It is a very somber tale of obsession. She never understood that the beauty and grace that she was seeking was to be found on the inside, in her soul. Grass always withers and flowers always fade, aah, but the soul, my friend, goes on and on. Why some creatures spend all their time on the shell and not enough time on the peanut, well, I'll never know. Poor Narcy. I had such high hopes for her." Badger paused to stir the silver once more, then continued, "Remember, tiny traveler, purity of the soul is only achieved through trials; and soon you'll be ready when *you* have been tested by fire."

Corky was careful to ponder the words of wisdom from Badger. The trade was soon completed, and the farewells and blessings were passed about freely.

"Farewell, wee travelers!" shouted Badger. "As you slide down the banister of life, may the splinters never be pointing the wrong way."

"Farewell, Badger!" shouted Captain Nibbles. "May your troubles be as few and far apart as my granny's teeth." They all laughed and waved before the hamsters were on their way again. Even though they did not find a freshwater spring to bring water back to the other hamsters, they left with thirty ironwood and silver-tipped needle arrows with colorful quetzal feathered flights, along with nine silver daggers and a large bobbin of sturdy fishing line. The company of badgers feasted on juice-drippy pears for many, many days. The sweet pear juice made them all dizzy with joy and satisfaction. The hamsters returned to Fort Chewy later that day after a successful journey to find food and weapons. The entire fort feasted and grew plumpy-full before falling asleep under the light of a brilliant moon.

Chapter 6

A Berry Deep Sleep

The sun was an early morning flower, bursting open with a golden glow. The first streaks of sunlight pierced the tiny openings in the wicker walls of the basket fort, leaving squares of light on the fur of the sleeping hamsters. Skittles blinked his eyes open to try to force himself awake. There was an empty space next to him where Wendell Cheeks had been sleeping. The absence of Wendell's warm body woke Skittles. He looked across the sea of fur, all rising and falling as they slept under a checkered blanket of light. He looked past the sleeping hamsters and saw that the door of the fort was open.

"Wendell! Where are you?" Skittles whisper-shouted loud enough to wake up at least ten of the nearest hamsters. They started to stir and mutter garbled questions since they were still half asleep.

"Who's missing!" cried Mr. Whiskers.

"Blimey! Who left the blasted gate open?" yelled Cletus.

"Will someone tell me what is going on?" Captain Nibbles boomed. By now, all the hamsters in Fort Chewy were awake, some still wiping the sleep from their eyes. Skittles made his way through a small crowd to stand in front of Captain Nibbles to report the distressing news.

"Captain Nibbles, sir," he said excitedly. "I believe... Wendell Cheeks is missing! I fell asleep, listening to his ham-snoring last night; and when I woke up, he had vanished!"

"What do you mean *vanished*?" Captain Nibbles replied.

"He's gone, sir. There's no sign of him. We found the door of the fort unsecured. He must have left the basket!" There was panic and fear in Skittle's voice. He was clearly distraught as he gave his report.

Captain Nibbles seemed to be deep in thought for a moment, then issued an order. "We will assemble a search party, and we *will* find Wendell Cheeks!" promised the captain. "Chewy, Two-Spots, Corky, and Buttercup, prepare to search for our lost brother."

Buttercup stumbled forward blindly and addressed Captain Nibbles. "Permission to be excused, Captain," requested Buttercup. His eyelids seemed to be stuck together, and he couldn't look directly at the captain.

"I see that you are suffering from sticky eye, a common malady that moves among us," answered the captain. "Yes, Buttercup, you are excused from this detail." He then asked Puff Bottom and Cheerio to attend to Buttercup's needs to help restore his sight.

Just as they were leading Buttercup away, a volunteer quickly stepped forward. "I will go in his place, sir," offered a voice from the crowd.

"Step forward, young hamster," ordered the captain. "What is your name?"

"I am Toby, the son of Hugo Von Schnee. My full name is Tobias Von Schnee, a member of a noble Bavarian hamster clan, but here I am just called Toby. The other hamsters didn't seem to want to associate with a hamster of *privilege and nobility*, as Chewy explained to me. He thought that 'Toby' would be a name that common hamsters could relate to. Plus it's much easier to remember. I was a member of the Royal Bavarian Archery Brigade, and I am quite proficient with a bow and arrow," said Toby with pride. "I am the holder of the Hamsterbecher trophy three years running." He straightened himself and puffed out his chest.

"Very impressive, young Toby. We *could* use your skills in our search for Wendell Cheeks. Welcome aboard!" the captain said invitingly. To complete the search party, Captain Nibbles knew that he also needed hamsters blessed with olfactory skills. The sisters were standing close, and Captain Nibbles was aware of their skills.

"I want you to come with us, Lola and Rosie," the captain continued. "I've heard that you are both excellent trackers. Your sniffers are very impressive, and your smelling skills are legendary!"

"Are you sure you want ladies on this mission, Captain? Remember, *glasses and lasses are fragile ware*," said Sassypants.

"I'll show you fragile!" squealed Lola, as she moved toward Sassypants.

"Enough!" cried Captain Nibbles. "We must prepare to leave the safety of the basket."

Captain Nibbles gathered the search party closer and spoke to them. "We will not lose one of our own. If you are too frightened to go on this dangerous mission, speak up now. There is no shame if your fear is greater than your will to serve."

"What if Wendell just had to *spend a penny*?" asked Two-Spots.

"What do you mean *spend a penny*?" asked Captain Nibbles.

"You know, visit the loo, find the dunny, heed the call of nature," answered Two-Spots.

Chewy stepped in and tried to help explain the term to Captain Nibbles. "He's trying to say…that maybe…Wendell just left the fort to find a potty."

"I see," answered the captain. "Well, we'll find out soon. Prepare to leave the fort. And maybe you should all *spend a penny* before we leave."

The search party was ready to travel in a matter of minutes. They were now assembled and waiting to exit through the gate. Chewy, Two-Spots, Corky, Toby, Lola, and Rosie had readied themselves to venture into the wild to find Wendell Cheeks. And Captain Nibbles was ready to lead them.

Chadwick the Holy came through the crowd to offer a blessing. "May your whiskers and sniffers be sharp and strong. And may your heart be even stronger. May the dreams you hold dearest be those that come true, and the kindness you spread, keep returning to you. May wisdom guide you and good favor rest upon you. May you find success against your enemies; and may our brother, Wendell, return to us unharmed. We wish you all the mercies of heaven. Haste ye back."

A low and steady snore could be heard as Two-Spots fell asleep during the blessing. Corky nudged him awake with a sharp jab of his elbow. Chadwick the Holy bowed to the captain after his blessing and retreated into the crowd of gathered hamsters. As the search party filed through the gate into the unknown, Captain Nibbles yelled back, "Bar the gate! Secure the fort!" The gate closed, and the search party disappeared into the forest to search for their lost brother.

The search team traveled all day, and the blazing sun was causing the forest to dampen and sweat. Rivulets of steam rose upward from the forest floor. The rescuers were weary and famished. They were absolutely hollow with hunger. Captain Nibbles could see the exhaustion in their faces and decided it would be best for all of them to rest for the night. They sat down in a protective circle, facing outwardly, the same way bobwhites sleep at night to protect their flock from predators. *Learn from the birds of the air*, Captain Nibbles would often say. Lola and Rosie noticed a delightful bush with luscious berries less than ten feet away from their circle.

"Berries!" squealed Lola.

"Why, I'll be gobsmacked!" Corky said excitedly.

"Innit beautiful!" Rosie marveled while gazing upon the berry-filled bush.

"What kind of berries are they?" asked Corky.

"Too hungry to care!" shouted Two-Spots, rubbing his furry belly. All at once the circle broke, and seven famished hamsters gathered tightly around a helpless berry bush. Even though they couldn't identify the berries, they devoured them anyway. The fur around their nibbling mouths was wet, matted down, and stained purple. They chew-slurped the berries to their hearts' content. The hamsters continued to eat until their bellies swelled with satisfaction. After they guzzle-gobbled the last of the berries, they were ready to lie down for the night. As they lay on their backs under the star-flooded sky, the hamsters were so stuffed that their bellies looked like casaba melons quite ready for harvest. They drifted off into a deep and dreamy sleep. It was like falling in slow motion into a large black hole, but never reaching the bottom. They fell deeper and deeper and even deeper into a dark cave of emptiness, not knowing that the berries had caused their heavy slumber.

It was still dark when the effect of the berries began to wear off. The captain was the first to begin waking up. He was quite groggy and disoriented when he opened his eyes. His heart began beating faster as he sat up and realized that he was waking up in a strange and threatening place. He and the other hamsters were helpless captives in a locked black iron cage! He vigorously shook the other hamsters awake.

As they slowly fought off the effects of the berries, they looked around in confusion. Surrounded by rusty metal bars, the hamsters thought they were in the middle of a nightmare. When they became fully awake, a cold panic crawled over their skin. Captain Nibbles remembered stories of how the wolves would try to control the will of the forest animals. He suspected that the wolves had planted the sleep berry bushes throughout the forest to keep the animals sluggish and confused. It was just another way that Serigala, king of the wolves, ruled his corrupt kingdom through trickery and deception. Whoever discovered the hamsters in such a deep state of sleep must have dragged them to this prison. Was it the wolves or someone else?

Chapter 7

One Lost Hamster

Rosie alerted the others with a sudden fearful shout. "It's Wendell Cheeks!" shrieked Rosie. Everyone looked out through the bars of the cage to a large open campfire with climbing flames. Close to the fire stood Wendell Cheeks, tied to a post stuck firmly in the ground. He looked terribly frightened and alone. Sitting near the blazing campfire were three massive wild boars, each one fatter and uglier than the next. They were squatting on logs like arrogant kings, all laughing and snorting uncontrollably. Their smell wafted through the air in the direction of the cage where the hamster prisoners were confined. A few of the hamsters began to gag from the stench of the feral hogs.

"Devil pigs!" Captain Nibbles said in a dark, troubling tone. "Their tusks are as sharp as razors and can slice your flesh to ribbons. They have hooves that can trample you into dust. But even more frightening, they have no conscience or soul." The boars were loud and vulgar, making gruesome sounds. Their snortings were deep, foul, and thunderous.

"I fear they are preparing to snack on poor Wendell Cheeks," cried Two-Spots. "I'm sure that he is the sampler, and we are the belly fillers."

"Check for your weapons," ordered Captain Nibbles. The hamsters searched for their bows, arrows, and daggers. Not finding them, they looked outside the cage to see them stacked in a jumbled pile. They were just out of reach, which made them useless.

"We must act fast!" warned Captain Nibbles. "Lola, can you squeeze through those bars? We must get to our weapons." He asked Lola because she was the slightest of all the hamsters and very limber.

"I'll try, Captain," Lola answered. She immediately moved closer to the cage bars and stuck her left foot through two of the bars, then her leg. She sucked in her slight furry belly, then wiggled, twisted, and pushed until she popped out on the other side of the cage. She immediately scampered to the front of the cage where she shimmied up to a latch that secured the prison door. She lifted it with all her might. She was stronger than anyone thought, and it squeaked open to their surprise. There was a stifled cheer from the hamsters below since they didn't want to alert the wild hogs. From the inside, the hamsters used their weight to push against the heavy metal door until it was open just enough to allow even the chubbiest hamster to fit through. And if Two-Spots could fit through, they could all fit through. The prisoners filed out of the cage quickly, passing through the door to freedom. They crept silently to the bows, arrows, and daggers that were tossed into a twisted, tangled heap. The archers quickly armed themselves and readied their silver-tipped arrows. The band of furry fugitives slipped away from the cage and hid in a line of trees that surrounded the camp of the wild boars. The hogs were too busy being rowdy and repulsive to notice that the cage that held the hamsters was now empty. The furry warriors had escaped and were now hiding behind the cover of trees on the edge of their camp.

"What are we going to do? I fear that Wendell is going to slide down their slimy gullets!" Corky whispered with obvious fear in his voice.

"We came to find Wendell Cheeks; and we will bring him home, uncooked, unchewed, and unswallowed," Captain Nibbles promised all the hamsters with assurance.

"The first order of business," said the captain with confidence, "is to walk right in the middle of their camp and order those foul, disgusting tusky rooters to let our Wendell go. Then I am going to march right out of there, untouched, with Wendell by my side." The hamsters looked at each other thinking that Captain Nibbles's mind had gone all dotty.

"And just what will *we* be doing, Captain?" asked Rosie.

"Gather close, hamster champions. Here's the plan." Captain Nibbles whispered the plan so the black-hearted tusky rooters would not overhear him.

The fire was now hot enough and quite ready to roast a tasty hamster snack. The three wild boars, Dingus, Butkus, and Sir Walter Fat Belly, were puffy-full from rooting and grazing all day; but they were quite ready for some sweet and dainty afters by the campfire. Walter seemed to be the boss of the three as he was shouting all the orders.

"Dat fire is plenty hot and ready! Get dat rat on da spit!" ordered Sir Walter, as pig slobber drip-splashed from his tusks. "And after I strip the meat from *his* bones, you bring me those other fancy rats from the meaty cage." He sat back scratching his fat, hairy belly with his front hooves. Then he started sing-snorting a dark and ugly song while he clapped his back hooves together.

> Hammy meat, Hammy treat,
> Bite off his head
> And spit out his feet

"Aye, Sir Walter," answered Dingus. "He's a plumpy beaut, he is. I'll grabs him off da post. He'll be crispy fried in the eye of a bat!"

"It's *the bat* of an *eye*, you moron," corrected Butkus.

"You is a moron…you…moron," shot back Dingus.

"Enough!" bellowed Sir Walter. "I need sweet, sweet hamster meat," he said with flies buzzing around his greasy, hairy body. Then they all started chanting as Dingus led Wendell Cheeks to the firepit.

> Sweet meat, tasty treat,
> Bite off his head
> And spit out his feet!

THE LOST HAMSTERS OF BARNABY BUNCH

Spit out his feet
And bite off his head,
Chew him all up
Until he's all dead!

Captain Nibbles stepped out from the shadow of the trees. Before he entered the camp of the enemy, he heard the still small voice of Barnaby Bunch whisper, "Trust the flame stone." The captain reached into his pocket and pulled out the small leather pouch. He opened it and poured the five stones into his hand and plucked out the red flame stone. He clutched it tightly as he put the remaining stones back into the pouch before sliding it back into his inside vest pocket. Captain Nibbles walked right into the middle of the camp, while the devilish laughing and snorting from the arrogant wild pigs continued. The wee hamster came face-to-face with the three brutish hogs as he held the stone firmly in his tiny fist.

"Greetings, gentlemen! What a splendid-looking group of tusky rooters we have here," articulated Captain Nibbles.

"Looky what we haves here," Sir Walter Fat Belly scoffed, as he scratched his haunches with a hoof. The three wild boars were shocked and amused that another hamster had sauntered into their private camp, bold as can be. Walter continued, "The question that I be askin' myself is, why would a plumpy, fluffy circus rat be wanderin' all alone on the darkest of nights?"

Captain Nibbles was calm and unruffled as he faced the three huge beasts. "Oh, I'm not wandering, Mr. Fat Belly, and I'm not alone. I'm here to rescue my friend and brother. His name is Wendell Cheeks. That's Wendell right there, the one you have tied to a post," Captain Nibbles said without emotion. The three boars looked at each other and broke out into an evil snorting laugh.

"Well, the way we sees it...," Sir Walter responded, "is that we now have one more tasty treat to munch and swallows. You are makin' my mouth go all slip-drippy. We'll just adds you to da meaty cage over there."

"You mean that hamster-empty cage over there?" asked Captain Nibbles. The three boars quickly looked over at the vacant cage with the open door, then back at Captain Nibbles, wondering what was going on. The captain continued, "It might be rather difficult for you to enjoy a hamster picnic when you are dealing with all the pain."

"What pain?" the three repulsive brutes said in unison.

"The sharp pain of a silver-tipped arrow shot inside your ear," Captain Nibbles answered with an unflappable calmness in his voice.

"Our ears is fine as horse feathers," boasted Sir Walter. "Throw that smarty-pants ball of fur on the fire with the small one," he ordered Dingus and Butkus. They moved toward Captain Nibbles to grab him, when suddenly, Captain Nibbles raised the red flame stone, then heaved it right into the middle of their blazing firepit. Immediately the flames died down for a moment, and the firepit became quiet and still. Then a low rumbling could be heard like the sound of a distant earthquake. It grew louder and louder until suddenly, brightly colored firebrands began to shoot out of the firepit, aimed directly at the boars. Red-hot missiles of burning coals landed at their feet, causing them to perform twitchy, awkward dances. Scorched tails and hooves sent the boars into a chaotic frenzy. As they ran in big circles to avoid the shooting firebrand missiles, they crashed into each other, causing great pain.

While Captain Nibbles witnessed the flame stone's power, he yelled at the top of his lungs, "ARCHERS, NOTCH! ARCHERS, DRAW! ARCHERS, LOOSE!"

Tiny needle arrows with silver tips shot out from the trees, whistling through the air toward the boars. A sharp arrow sailed through the night air and stuck fast inside Sir Walter's right ear. He let out a terrific snort and howl! The first arrow was quickly followed by a second, finding its mark inside the left ear of Butkus. Everything went dark and dizzy for Dingus as he felt a painful stab inside his left snout hole. The hogs were all screeching and snorting and hop-hobbling around the campfire as the arrow attack continued. The disgusting beasts began to dash away from the campsite in utter pain when the hamsters fired another round of ironwood arrows, striking the tusky rooters square on their mangy rumps. The hogs scurried away from the camp to escape deeper into the forest, snort-howling as they scrambled away in scorching pain. The hamsters erupted into a collective shout of victory and emerged from the trees to celebrate with Captain Nibbles and Wendell Cheeks. What a sight to behold! They watched three giant hairy wild boars with arrows firmly stuck in their ears, snout holes, and portly duffs, running for their pathetic lives. Lola quickly ran to Wendell to untie him from the post. Wendell's eyes flooded with tears as he hugged Captain Nibbles first, then all his friends. He thought he was about to die, and his friends snatched him from the flames.

Who are these misfit hamsters that would risk their lives for an insignificant creature like me? Wendell Cheeks thought.

The captain gathered the seven proud hamsters and told them about the five stones and the *Songs of Light* that had been given to him by Barnaby. They were all overwhelmed with full, thankful hearts, and of course, a thousand questions. Even though Barnaby was not with them in person, he was still helping them on their journey. For the first time, Captain Nibbles was convinced that he and the other hamsters were being called to do something far greater, but rescuing one lost hamster was a magnificent beginning.

Chapter 8

The Rapids

The hamsters were resting next to the smoldering fire that the boars had made to cook Wendell Cheeks. They were enjoying their victory by comparing their bow skills and sharp aim. They laughed at how the boars fled in anguish and pain. Captain Nibbles interrupted their celebration to remind them it was only one victory and that there would be many more battles ahead. He cautioned them to be humble and thankful for today's victory, but to remain watchful for new dangers. The hamsters immediately tempered their jubilation, at least in the captain's presence. But some of them still couldn't hide their excitement completely.

As the captain walked away, Corky whispered to the others rather enthusiastically, "Did you *see* that arrow fly? Whoooosh! I got him smack in the snout hole! Bull's-eye and jackpot!" There were a few nervous giggles because they knew the captain was right. It was only one victory.

Captain Nibbles took Wendell aside from the others to talk to him privately.

"Wendell, I'm going to be short on the sugar," said the captain candidly. "Why did you leave the basket fort in the first place? Because of you, I had to assemble a search party, which put us all in great danger."

"For that I am very, very sorry, Captain," Wendell answered. "But look at me, Captain. I am a scrawny, homely creature. I was the runt of my litter, an undesirable throwaway. Nothing about me is memorable."

"Which does not answer my question," said Captain Nibbles. "Why did you leave Fort Chewy?"

"Water," replied Wendell. The fort is dry as a bone, and I thought if I found a cool stream or a fresh spring, I would be a hero. I'd be a somebody."

"So you really weren't thinking about the others, were you?" said the captain. "You speak about how low *you* are, how scrawny *you* are, how undesirable *you* are, what a throwaway *you* are. That is not humility—that is pride wearing a mask. All that talk is just more of you thinking about yourself."

"But I *do* want to be a hero. I *do* want to be useful to others," Wendell cried.

"Wendell, stop *thinking less of yourself* and start *thinking of yourself less*. Then you will know humility," the captain said wisely. Wendell Cheeks walked back to his friends at the campfire, still pondering the captain's words.

The hamsters continued to quietly celebrate their victory long into the night. As the embers of the campfire continued to smolder, they grew very tired. The popping sound of charred logs mixed with the steady rhythm of Two-Spots's snoring and nose whistling caused them to drift peacefully asleep.

When the first light of the sun gloriously broke the horizon, the hamsters slowly began to stir and stretch. They all gradually woke up except for Two-Spots, who was still dead to the world. Loud snores were still rumbling from underneath his blanket. The coals from the fire were still warm, and a few of the hamsters were gathering around it to soak up the last of its gentle waves of heat.

When the hamsters were all fed and packed up, they were ready to leave Camp Devil Pig, as Captain Nibbles called it. They tromped and footslogged along forest trails for hours before settling down for a rest. They dozed, snacked, and dozed some more. During a late afternoon rest, the hamsters became engaged in a rather senseless conversation about who could fit the most sunflower seeds in their cheeks. Rosie thought it was a very immature boy-hamster thing to brag about, and she told them so. She was scolding them sternly when Captain Nibbles walked up and pleaded for silence, which led to an end of all the ham-chattering.

"Listen!" he said. "I hear something. What do you make of it, Corky?"

Corky's ears perked up to listen closer. After a quiet moment, he replied, "It's a river, sir. It seems to be coming from just beyond that donut peach tree grove." Corky's ears perked up and began twitching. He continued to listen closely before speaking again. "Definitely a river, sir, with very angry waters. Fifty feet across. And…a thunderous waterfall." Corky's listening skills were nothing short of remarkable.

Two-Spots didn't care much about river talk. As soon as he heard the words *donut peach trees*, he began thinking about biting into the luscious, sweet donut peaches, with the juice dripping off his elbows. Sometimes he had trouble focusing on the matter at hand and could easily disappear into his own thoughts. Chewy said that when Two-Spots started thinking about food, he was off with the fairies. Sometimes it took quite a while for him to come back.

Captain Nibbles ordered his band of hamster explorers to pack up so they could explore the river. As they walked past the trees, Two-Spots reached up to pluck a few of the low-hanging peaches. The hamster scouts soon found themselves on a rocky bluff overlooking a mighty, rushing river. The white-capped waves seemed enraged and unpredictable. They all gazed in wonder at the turbulent, churning river. They were in awe of its pure force and energy.

Within seconds, their gaze turned upriver to witness, with horror, a mother duck named Webbelyn and her five ducklings quacking frantically. They were desperately trying to navigate the speeding waves. The terrified ducks tried to steer themselves with their webbed feet, but they were no match for the violent, swirling waters beneath them. The ducklings were no longer in a line behind their mother, as the force of the river drove them apart. The loving family of ducks was now scattered and separated from one another. Now, it was every duck for himself. The speed of the river quickly increased as it spilled angrily over sharp rocks. The ducks could not see ahead or even imagine their impending doom, but the hamsters could see from the height of the riverbank that a monstrous, swallowing waterfall awaited them. The ducks would be swept over the edge in a matter of minutes.

"Archers, get ready! Chewy, take Two-Spots, Toby, and Corky! Run ahead and secure a rescue line! You'll know what to do! And take Wendell Cheeks with you! Go, GO, GO!" cried Captain Nibbles. They scampered as if their tails were on fire, racing ahead of the enraged river. They jumped over tree roots and zigzagged through brambles, as the raging river flowed below them. Captain Nibbles, Rosie, and Lola would meet them at the riverbank, just above the falls, before the water spilled over its edge. The archers dash-darted ahead and stopped when they found a clearing. Each of them began to fasten their needle arrows to the fishing line that Badger had given them. They tied one end of the line around nearby tree trunks. The other end was tied to their arrows. Hopefully they had correctly judged the distance across the river and had enough fishing line to reach the other side. Toby, the bow master, was crucial in helping the others calculate the distance.

"What should *I* do?" screamed Wendell.

"After we hit our marks, we'll need your help in the rescue!" yelled Chewy.

"I hope you are not afraid of water, Wendell Cheeks!" shouted Corky over the deafening noise of the rushing water. The flailing and thrashing ducks were getting closer.

"Ducks on the water!" shouted Two-Spots.

"Notch!" roared Chewy. The archers placed their arrows in their bows. "Draw!" yelled Chewy seconds later. They pulled back their strings and aimed their arrows. The four archers carefully held their aim at tree targets across the river. "Loose!" shouted Chewy. The four needle arrows shot across the river with great force. They whistled over the surface of the water with great speed, barely inches above the angry waves. *Thppp, thppp, thppp, thppp.* All four arrows hit their mark, burying themselves securely into the trunks of sturdy trees across the river. The archers had estimated the distance perfectly, so the wires were taut between the trees on both sides of the river. The four archers began to carefully crawl across the lifelines, hand over hand, with legs locked over the wires, to the center of the river. They hovered only inches above the angry rushing water. Wendell watched the others, then followed. The fast-moving water rushed underneath them as they grasped tightly to the thread of life. The five hamsters were spread out and positioned to grab the passing ducks before they sailed over the edge of the raging waterfall. Wendell clung to a lifeline and had a sudden thought that this might be his moment. This was his chance to rise up; this was his chance to be a hero!

The five hamsters had their legs wrapped around the fishing line while they leaned upside down very close to the rushing water's surface, waiting for the ducks to flow just beneath them. The first duckling to reach the hamsters was snatched up by Chewy. The duckling was gathered up into Chewy's arms and held tightly. Next, it was Toby. As a duckling thrashed in the water beneath him, Toby reached down and almost lost his grip but was able to gather himself to grab the duckling before it was swallowed by the monstrous waterfall. Corky grabbed a third duckling and snatched him out of the water while directing Webbelyn to latch on to the fishing wire with her beak. She was far too large to lift out of the water, but her beak was strong enough to lock on to the line so she could wait to be towed to shore. Two-Spots was in position to rescue a duckling but instead was slapped in the face by the tail of a very rude butterfish before the fish disappeared over the waterfall. Two-Spots had many skills, but rescuing ducklings was not one of them.

Wendell Cheeks was the only hamster left to try to save the last two ducklings before they met their death. The baby ducks were flowing rapidly toward Wendell, and he wasn't sure how he could save them both. He had one hand on the line and one hand reaching down close to the water. The ducklings were terrified and felt hopeless as they came closer to Wendell's outstretched hand. Just as the two ducklings reached closer to his grasp, Wendell's hand that held on to the line slipped, and he fell into an upside-down position with the top of his head bobbing in and out of the rushing river. The ducklings crashed into Wendell, knocking him loose from the lifeline and into the water. Now Wendell *and* the two ducklings were headed straight for the waterfall, bobbing like corks in the water. Wendell

Cheeks was no longer thinking about being a hero, only how all three of them were going to survive. As they moved closer to the edge of the furious waterfall, Wendell knew that there were only a few seconds left. He opened his mouth as wide as he could, grabbed hold of one duckling, and shoved the terrified duckling inside his left cheek. As the first duckling was secured inside Wendell's puffed-out cheek, Wendell reached out through the speeding water and grabbed the tail feathers of the second tiny duck. In one swift motion, he stuffed the petrified duckling into his right cheek. Wendell had been searching so long for his special gift that he forgot that all hamsters have the amazing natural ability to expand their own cheeks in case of emergency. Both ducklings were securely squeezed into Wendell's cheeks, but they were now at the very edge of the raging waterfall. The violent white water swallowed Wendell with the two baby ducks inside his cheeks, like an angry giant, chewing and swallowing his breakfast. Wendell disappeared over the raging waterfall while the rest of the hamsters watched in total disbelief and horror. Wendell Cheeks was now gone, swallowed by a cold, heartless avalanche of water.

Webbelyn was in total anguish as she watched two of her little ones disappear over the edge. The hamsters all bowed their heads in respect, for in *their* eyes, Wendell was a true hero for his attempt to save others. Captain Nibbles was very distraught as he watched from the shore. He took out the green life stone from his pocket. He looked down at the word *life* written on the surface of the stone. With tears in his eyes and unimaginable sorrow in his heart, he angrily threw the green stone as hard as he could into the rampaging river. The angry river mocked him as it simply swallowed the stone whole, letting it sink in its churning waters. Wendell Cheeks and the two ducklings were gone. The captain was angry with himself for not remembering to use the life stone sooner. *Now it is too late*, he thought.

Chewy, Toby, and Corky inched their way back to the riverbank, holding tight to the fishing line, each carrying a shivering and very frightened duckling. Two-Spots came back with a bright-red mark on his cheek from being severely fish-slapped by the butterfish. They held fast to the lifeline and used what strength they had left to move closer to the riverbank where Captain Nibbles and the sisters were waiting to help pull them to dry land. Webbelyn inched closer to the riverbank as well, although she had to let the line slide between her duck bill as she paddled sideways to greet the others. When they reached the safety of the bank and were helped out by the waiting hamsters, they all collapsed on solid ground. It was a bittersweet reunion as they were relieved that they were alive, yet their hearts were filled with ache and sorrow from losing Wendell Cheeks and the two precious ducklings. Sometimes there are no words to describe the depths of sorrow and despair you feel when you lose someone you love.

Captain Nibbles spoke first, his voice cracking a bit. "Wendell Cheeks died to save others. He had the heart of a hero." The captain wiped tears from his red eyes, then continued, "We should hike down to the bottom of the falls and gather our fallen hero…and those two brave little ducklings." Webbelyn emitted a frightful wail and was impossible to console. The hamsters knew this was going to be the most difficult thing that they would ever have to do. But they all stood up and prepared to hike down the steep, brambly ravine that led to the bottom of the waterfall. They weren't even sure if they would ever find poor Wendell. The river was savage and merciless and had probably already carried Wendell and the ducklings far downstream.

They reached the bottom of the falls to see water crashing and foaming. Within the spray of the water, a brilliant rainbow appeared that stretched across the river.

Sharp rocks jutted out of the water, creating a sick feeling in Captain Nibbles's stomach. They all stopped, both hamsters and ducks, as if assembling for an unplanned moment of silence. The crash of the waves against the rocks seemed to taunt them as their hearts throbbed with sorrow.

It didn't seem like the torture of agony would end, when they all heard it at once. Mixed in with the sound of water crashing upon the rocks, they could all hear a faint and very weak "Quaaack…" At first, they looked at the three small ducklings gathered at the feet of Webbelyn, but the ducklings all insisted that it wasn't them that quacked. Rosie jumped up and down as she squealed loudly. She was the first to notice Wendell lying face up on a rock along the bank.

"Over there! On that rock! It's Wendell!" she cried. They all looked over to where she was pointing. Just downstream under a low-hanging branch along the bank, they saw a small ball of fur, belly up, lying on a smooth flat river rock. They all scurried toward Wendell as quickly as they could. As they approached, they looked down at his tiny body, hoping for any sign of life, but they found none.

"He looks colder than a codfish," observed Corky.

"Why are his cheeks so puffy?" questioned Chewy.

They had all surrounded him, watching and waiting. Then suddenly, they all witnessed the tiny head of a duckling popping out of Wendell's mouth. His quacking became louder and stronger. As they gathered around Wendell, who looked very blue and still, Lola grabbed a stick and gently poked his puffed-up belly. As soon as she did this, the duckling popped right out of Wendell's mouth, fluttered his wings, and landed softly at the feet of his mama. Then wonder of all wonders, a second duckling head popped out of Wendell's mouth. The startled duckling looked around and couldn't understand why everyone was weeping. After a long moment, he let out a terrific "Quaaaack!" as if to say, "Stop crying and get me out of this hamster's mouth!"

Lola poked Wendell's bloated tummy once again, and out popped the second duckling! He flapped his wings wildly, then landed gently on top of Rosie's head. Rosie reached up and carefully took the confused duckling into her small hands. She walked over and placed him carefully at Webbelyn's feet. Webbelyn's tears were now flowing from a deep well of joy and thanksgiving. She was thankful that all her little ones were now alive and safe, but she was also thankful for Wendell's selfless act of heroism. His quick thinking saved her children, and she would never forget his act of courage. Tears welled up in the eyes of all the hamsters as they witnessed the reunion of a joyful mother and her precious children.

The flow of their tears stopped when they heard the sudden sound of coughing and sputtering. They looked back at Wendell in complete astonishment as they saw him spitting and choking up river water. They rushed back and surrounded his small soaked body. Wendell's natural color was beginning to return to his furry cheeks. As they looked down at him in disbelief, his eyes opened just a crack, and he quietly uttered, "Lola, if *you* poke my belly one more time…"

"He's alive!" Two-Spots shouted. He was so excited that when he fell upon Wendell's frail body to hug him, more river water shot out of poor Wendell's mouth like a fountain.

"Miracle of miracles!" Corky shouted. He was clearly flummoxed *and* flabbergasted. They were all shocked and overwhelmed. Lola and Rosie knelt to help Wendell slowly sit up. After a few moments, they gently helped him up and held on to him until his sea legs stopped wobbling. Wendell Cheeks once was dead, but now he was alive!

Captain Nibbles felt a deep shame that he doubted the power of the *life stone*. But his shame melted away when he took Wendell's small face in his two hands, looked in his eyes, and said, "Today is your hero day, Wendell Cheeks."

Chapter 9

Castello del Lupo (Wolf Castle)

It was a very long, heart-pounding day, and the hamsters were tattered and frazzled. Every ounce of their strength was drained. A decision was made to camp by the side of the river for the night. It was time for the ducks to say farewell after many heartfelt thanks and hugs. They paddled down the relaxed river under the soft light of the moon as a family once again. This time the ducklings swam much closer to their mama, Webbelyn. Chewy and Corky built a very satisfying fire that warmed the hamsters' chilled and knackered bodies. They gathered around the dazzling flames, munching on a late-night snack of beetroot and jackfruit seeds. Soon, sleep conquered them all, and they surrendered to its gentle call.

In the middle of the night, the wolves arose to worship the moon. Their sinister howls seemed alarmingly loud and closer this time. The vibrations of their howls shook the branches of the trees around the hamster camp. Even Two-Spots woke up. Every howl seemed to echo off the rocks near them, causing fear to spread like a lightning fire. The hamsters were all looking to Captain Nibbles for comfort and encouragement, but they noticed that his legs were trembling as well. The brilliant moon drifted behind a great wall of darkening clouds, and the dreadful howling soon turned into silence.

The hamster explorers soon slipped back into an unsettled sleep, but even that didn't last long.

An impending feeling of doom woke Lola first. What she saw through the remaining flickers of the campfire absolutely paralyzed her. In the shadows stood a massive and savage wolf. He looked fierce, powerful, and hungry. The great beast stood motionless, just watching the sleeping hamsters. His mouth was open, revealing very sharp, dripping teeth. Lola couldn't speak. Her mouth was dry, and her throat had closed shut. She stared at the wolf, and he glared back at her with a ghastly stare. She somehow found the ability to give Chewy, who was asleep next to her, a firm kick in his side. He stirred, blinked his eyes open, and followed Lola's blank stare at the wolf. Chewy in turn elbowed Corky awake, and Corky poked Wendell until he woke up. Wendell gave Two-Spots a sharp jab to wake him out of his deep sleep. The hamsters never took their eyes off the wolf, mesmerized by the most incredible beast they had ever seen. He could have attacked and swallowed them whole before they could even make a move. But he didn't. He just stared at them with murder in his yellow eyes.

Captain Nibbles took one step forward. Even though he trembled, he tried to make his voice sound confident and fearless. "Who…are you…and what is your business here?" the captain asked cautiously.

A huge evil grin spread across the wolf's face as he answered, "Greetings, tiny rodents." He spoke deep and slow. "I am Nashoba. I have been sent from Castello del Lupo. You might know it as Wolf Castle." The hamsters were motionless and silent as they continued to listen to the fiendish, snarling wolf. Their biggest fear was that he would suddenly gobble them up in the blink of an eye.

"I was sent by the wolf king, our supreme leader, Serigala," the wolf declared. The hamsters continued to stare into the gaze of his penetrating eyes. They all began to fall into a deep and mindless trance as Nashoba continued to repeat his master's name, "Ser-i-ga-la, Ser-i-ga-la, Ser-i-ga-la…" By the time the name Serigala was spoken for the last time, the hamsters were all in a deep state of hypnosis. They stood frozen in their tracks with unblinking stares.

Captain Nibbles was the only one who remained unfazed by the wolf's tranquilizing power. He remembered reading in the *Songs of Light*, the book that Barnaby had given him, that those who were in love with the dark used every deception to try to control minds through trickery and deception. He was ready for the wolf's dark skills. While the wolf spoke, Captain Nibbles closed his eyes and silently repeated words and hummed melodies from the *Songs of Light*. The words seemed to cover his heart from the wolf's spellbinding voice. Nashoba continued to weave trickeries and confusion into the minds of the bewitched hamsters.

"You will now follow me to Wolf Castle," the dark wolf directed. "You will stand before the great Serigala. Gather your belongings. We leave now." Under his spell, the hamsters obeyed. They collected their rucksacks and made a single line facing the beguiling wolf. Captain Nibbles continued to pretend that he too was in a trance, following the directions of the wolf, for now. They began their obedient trek in the darkness toward the castle.

The monstrous wolf twisted along shadowy paths with eight hamsters following obediently behind him. They were on an unknown trail, led by a mind-controlling beast, to a diabolical castle that extinguishes every flicker of hope. Captain Nibbles was careful to memorize the path in case they would ever have an opportunity to escape. They journeyed to the castle during the darkest and loneliest hour of the night. Nighttime creatures scurried through the brush at their feet and huge hawk owls guarded the dark forest from their perches. They would have plummeted down to the ground to snatch the hamsters with their inescapable talons were it not for the menacing presence of Nashoba. The owls knew that these hamster prisoners were now the property of Serigala and Castello del Lupo, and they did not dare steal from the lord of the forest.

They marched in lockstep obedience for hours before they reached the base of the castle. When they arrived, Nashoba sat back on his haunches, tilted his head to the moonlit sky, and howled to signal the night watch wolves. A drawbridge began to lower with grinding creaks and moans from the movement of thick wood and bulky steel chains. The heavy drawbridge came to rest, after a terrific thud, over a ten-foot-wide moat that circled the castle. Captain Nibbles was almost overcome by the stench of the moat water. He had heard about the garderobes, toilets in the towers that were merely stone seats with a hole, hidden by a curtain. Garderobes emptied down long chutes straight into the moat. *It was good that the other hamsters were in a trance*, thought the captain. At least they didn't have to gag and wretch their way across the drawbridge.

Nashoba continued to walk across the heavy wooden bridge being closely followed by seven spellbound hamsters and Captain Nibbles. Standing inside the walls of the castle, the drawbridge was ordered to rise. The thick ancient door was raised slowly before shutting with a thunderous slam. The hamsters were now in the mouth of the castle and swallowed up by a heavy spirit of wickedness. For now, they belonged to Serigala, the dark wolf. They were *inside* the darkness, but the darkness was not *inside* of them.

Chapter 10

Welcome to the Oubliette

Once inside the castle, Nashoba led the hamsters into a wide-open courtyard. Captain Nibbles saw wolves everywhere. There were wolves snarling and gnashing at each other over scraps of raw meat. There were wolves chasing rats around the courtyard, trying to catch them before they barely escaped between the jagged cracks in the castle walls. There were wolves practicing their howling. But many of the wolves were like statues, staring at the hamsters as they marched by, their mouths open and dripping with hunger. As Captain Nibbles walked with the other hamsters, he was careful to observe anything that might help them survive. Nashoba led the hypnotized prisoners across the courtyard, past hungry, low-growling wolves. As they walked, Captain Nibbles looked up and noticed the four watchtowers. As he looked toward one of the towers, he locked eyes with the castle gyrfalcon, a magnificent bird of prey who seemed mesmerized by the hamsters, and Captain Nibbles in particular. He felt an immediate connection with the large falcon but didn't know why. He was also drawn to the Grand Tower, or the Keep, and he thought to himself that this must be where Serigala basked in his own evil.

Nashoba continued to lead the hamsters across the courtyard to the opposite side of the castle. A young gray wolf came close to the hamsters, sniffing and wondering what they would taste like, but Nashoba growled deeply as he bared his teeth to scare him away. When they reached the other side of the courtyard, they passed through the portcullis, a heavy door with spikes protruding from the bottom that could be dropped down to trap an enemy if they got inside the walls of the castle. After passing through this door, they were back inside a long stone hallway. As they continued down the dark passageway, Captain Nibbles saw light seeping through small openings in the wall. These were the arrow loops, or slits, made for archers to fire their stinging arrows at an approaching enemy. He looked up at the high ceiling and saw the murder holes, openings in the ceilings that the wolves could drop rocks or hot oil on invaders if they breached the castle walls during an attack. Wolf Castle was heavily fortified; and for the first time, Captain Nibbles could feel the darkness cover his soul like a heavy, smothering fog. He had a feeling they were being led to the oubliette, the dark place of the forgotten.

The oubliette had one entrance in the floor. Once you were dropped down through the caged door in the floor, you would look up to see that your only escape was now on the ceiling. It was the darkest and most hopeless place in the castle. Once there, your hope was crushed, and you were forgotten by the world. Captain Nibbles feared that this might be their final resting place. And yet his thoughts rebounded to wonder why Barnaby would send them here and give him the five stones if this was to be their end. A sliver of hope returned to him.

Each hamster was told to step into the open, gaping hole where they would fall to the cold, punishing floor below. Captain Nibbles maneuvered himself so he could go first. He strategically dropped his rucksack through the caged door to the floor below so he would have something softer to land on. After dropping through the hole and landing roughly, Chewy stepped obediently to the edge of the opening. He looked down into the darkness, then dropped through to the waiting floor. He landed on his back, but his rucksack broke the fall. Upon landing, the impact shook him out of his trance, and the hypnotic spell was broken. He stood up and looked with confusion at Captain Nibbles.

"Where are we? How did we get here?" Chewy asked in confusion. They both rubbed their damp fur and goose-bumpy skin to try to warm themselves.

"I'll explain later! The others are dropping! Help me!" cried Captain Nibbles.

One by one, the rest of the hamsters dropped down through the bleak oubliette portal. When the last hamster had dropped, the cold metal cage door was slammed shut, echoing throughout the dungeon. Each hamster was shaken out of their hypnotic trance as they dropped and hit the floor below. They all looked up at the ceiling and the closed trapdoor, their only means of escape. Captain Nibbles found the matches in his rucksack that Barnaby had given him. He struck one against the stone floor, then lit a torch that was fixed to the dungeon wall.

"Where…are we?" demanded Lola.

Captain Nibbles didn't try to hide the truth. "This, my friends, is our darkest hour. We've been led against our will to the castle of the wolves. We're captives of Serigala now. We're inside the oubliette, the dungeon of all dungeons.

"The *oubliette*. It means 'to forget,'" said Rosie with fear in her voice.

"Yes, Rosie," replied Captain Nibbles. "They want us to be locked away and forgotten forever. They call it the Ouboo. The wolves want to steal our will to live, to make us feel alone and forgotten by everyone. They want us to forget the light." The captain reached into his rucksack and pulled out the small leather book that he carried close to his heart. He leafed through the pages until he found what he was looking for. He coughed, then cleared his throat from the thick dust in the room. Then he began to read:

> In the middle of the darkest night
> When dreams away have flown,
> A soul in anguish slowly dies
> And withers all alone.

But amid the growing, bleak despair
A distant spark will glow,
The flame of life begins to burn
And hope is soon to grow.

After reading, Captain Nibbles looked around to see if anyone was beginning to feel a growing sense of hope. What he saw instead took his breath away. His closest friends and fellow warriors were beginning to physically disappear! Lola and Rosie were just beginning to disappear, while Two-Spots was nearly gone. Captain Nibbles could see the wall through Two-Spots's fading body. Their faces seemed to erase right in front of him. It was heartbreaking to watch. They all looked terrified and panic-stricken as they began to dissolve into thin air.

"Captain Nibbles, what is happening to us! I don't want to be forgotten. I want my life to mean something," Wendell said in despair.

"My body is vanishing!" Chewy screamed as he looked down to watch his own hands and arms slowly evaporate into air. "I'm a fading memory, a vapor!"

"I can't see my tummy or my feet, Captain!" cried Two-Spots, looking down. "I was a handsome, fuzzy hamster. Now I'm a ghost!" Every hamster except Captain Nibbles was slowly disappearing.

"I've never felt so alone!" cried Rosie. "Help us, Captain!"

"Listen, everyone! It's the spirit of the oubliette! It's causing you to vanish and be forgotten!" shouted the captain. The hamsters were so discouraged that they slowly lost their will to speak. Captain Nibbles could see that a veil of depression clouded the minds of the hamsters. The spirit of the oubliette was using the words of the light song against them, as the hamsters could only hear the *first part* of the song:

A soul in anguish slowly dies,
And withers all alone.

This was the very lowest that Captain Nibbles had ever seen his beloved companions, and now their bodies and souls were slipping away into a colorless vapor. There was nothing he could do to raise their spirits. His heavy body sank to the floor as he just watched his brothers slowly slip away into nothingness.

As the hamsters evaporated in despair, Captain Nibbles wondered why *he* wasn't disappearing. Then he remembered the stones tucked away inside his inner pocket.

Maybe the reason he wasn't vanishing was because the white hope stone was pressed against his heart. He fumbled for the pouch inside his inner pocket and pulled it out. He opened it and poured the remaining three stones into his hand. He could feel the words *water*, *light*, and finally *hope* etched into the stones. He clutched the yellow hope stone and put the others back in the pouch. He stood up with excitement and quoted the second part of the light song as loud as he could:

> But amid the growing, bleak despair
> A distant spark will grow,
> The flame of life begins to burn,
> And hope is soon to grow!

"Repeat the words, hamster warriors!" cried Captain Nibbles. "Let the song lift you up!" Seconds later, the captain heard the voices of seven invisible, frightened hamsters singing in the darkness of the oubliette.

"BUT AMID THE GROWING, BLEAK DESPAIR!" shouted Lola from a corner of the dungeon.

"A DISTANT SPARK WILL GROW!" yelled Toby from another corner.

"THE FLAME OF LIFE BEGINS TO BURN!" shouted Chewy from the empty darkness.

"AND HOPE IS SOON TO GROW!" exclaimed all the invisible hamsters together.

And at that moment, the captain heaved the hope stone with all his might against the prison wall. The stone struck the wall, sparking a thousand particles of light, which illuminated the oubliette. It became so bright that the hamsters' bodies slowly began to form and take shape again. Captain Nibbles could see them shielding their eyes from the bright explosion caused by the hope stone. He saw their feet reappearing first, then their legs, then their bellies, their chests, and then their happy, smiling faces. He was even thrilled to see the round fat belly of Two-Spots. The scattered particles of light that sparked from the stone remained glowing on the prison floor, continuing to chase the dark spirit of heaviness away. The hamsters stood in awe, looking down at their bodies once again, then looking at each other with unbridled joy.

"We will *not* be forgotten! Hope has saved us! This is not the end of us!" cried Wendell Cheeks.

"I've never been so happy to see all of you!" shouted Chewy.

"Something's wrong! I can't see my feet!" yelled Two-Spots.

"You've never been able to see your feet," answered Lola. "Your belly is blockin' the view," she added as all the hamsters laughed, including Two-Spots.

"And speakin' of my belly," added Two-Spots, "I need to fill it up with a tasty brambleberry tart right about now. Never thought I'd see another tart again."

Captain Nibbles approached the hamsters. "Hope brought you back today, my dear ones. It was hope that chased the dark spirit of the oubliette away, and it's the light of hope that will keep it away. You all made a choice for the moment, in desperation, but what do you choose for the rest of your days?"

"I choose to hope!" shouted Toby.

"I choose to hope!" yelled Lola.

"We choose to live in hope!" the hamsters cried out together.

"I choose dinner!" added Two-Spots, rubbing his belly. "I'm starving!" Everyone laughed at Two-Spots even though he was very serious. Captain Nibbles stood up and addressed the hamsters again.

"Two-Spots is right. Let's eat and renew our strength," shouted the captain. With that, every hamster pulled the last of the beetroots, seeds, and pears from their rucksacks. Soon their bellies ballooned like puffy, croak happy toads. They huddled together as one big ball of fur in order to keep warm in the bleak and freezing dungeon. As they all fell into a deep sleep, the only sounds within the dungeon were the gentle nose-wheezing of Two-Spots and, of course, *the rats*.

Chapter 11

Rat Bite Fever

The squealing of rats was both repulsive and terrifying. One of the castle rats sniff-wandered too close to the sleeping hamsters. His stiff whiskers brushed against Rosie, startling her out of a sound sleep. Her sudden movement vibrated through the other hamsters, waking them as well. They too became aware of the hideous squeaks and squeals of the rats, making them all quiver in fear, wondering if they were about to be attacked. The prisoners formed a circle of defense. The archers readied their bows and arrows, and the others had their daggers drawn. They all aimed outwardly into the darkness, waiting for an unseen enemy to attack.

"What...is...that abominable sound?" Corky whispered with a shaky voice.

"Rats!" declared Captain Nibbles.

They all stood on guard for what seemed an eternity, listening to the dreadful and horrifying sound of rats scurrying in the darkness, their clawlike nails scraping across the stone floor. The rats circled the shivering hamsters, chanting over and over with squealing voices,

> Just a little nibble
> Just a little peck,
> Rat Bite Fever
> When we bite you on the neck.

> Just a little nibble
> Or a big ratty bite,
> Gnawing on your bones
> In the middle of the night.

As the rats circled the hamsters, the squealing and scratching were sounds that gave them icy shivers, causing their blood to freeze. Captain Nibbles reached into his rucksack and slowly pulled out a matchstick. He struck the head of the match on the cold dungeon floor, and suddenly the dungeon walls danced with light and shadows from the flame. The rats immediately scurried to the darkest corners of the room, for rats love the darkness and fear the light. Captain Nibbles stepped out of the circle and held his matchstick out so the light would expose their strength and numbers. He counted thirty-three rats, all cowering against the dungeon walls, except one extremely large and gnarly rat. The gigantic rat did not move. This one must have been their leader as he possessed a confidence that the others lacked. Captain Nibbles gulped as he watched the monstrous rat inching closer to him.

"Ahoy, little puff. Tell me what name they might be callin' you?" asked the massive rodent.

"My name is…Nathaniel…Nibbles," answered the captain nervously. "My title is…Captain Nathaniel Nibbles, Esquire. I'm not *quite* a knight, but more than a gentleman. Somewhere between a gentleman and a knight, that is. I was born among the landed gentry, inheriting a country estate and manor, but sadly I found myself residing in Stumpy's Pet Shop, possibly due to a series of fateful circumstances, but more likely caused by countless poor decisions on my part, which to this day I woefully regret…" Captain Nibbles could hear that his words were out of control and made little sense, but he couldn't seem to help it. Standing before such a mammoth rodent gave him the jitter-shakes.

"I think you're overegging the pudding, little puff. I only wanted to know what name you answer to," repeated the rat. "We've heard tell of you, Mr. Nibbles. Your do-goody deeds have reached the earholes of every wretched bilge rat here in the castle." The bulky, giant rat flashed his sharp, pointy teeth while he talked. The hamsters cautiously listened as the giant rat continued, "We've also heard that you and your little fluffy puffies have even gotten the attention of the big wolf himself. Old Serigala has been growing mighty agitated with you, bringing all your sweetness and light into the forest. He *hates* sweetness and light, he does. We live here, inside the dark walls, and we hear everything. You know that the big wolf locked you in the old Ouboo so you and your friends would be lost and forgotten, you *and* your do-goody deeds. Nobody wants you speadin' all that happiness and honeydew around here. Savvy, mate? We're happy as clams here in the darkness. We don't need you coming in here and bodging up our enterprise, now, do we?"

"We didn't come to...*bodge up anyone's enterprise,* sir. We came to bring light and hope to a very dark forest. We are ready to face anything that stands in our way," said Captain Nibbles without fear. "Sir, I think *you* fear the light far more than *we* fear the darkness. By the way, how should I address you?" asked Captain Nibbles with renewed boldness.

"I am...Ratafia, the proud son of a bilge rat! My father was a bilge rat, and *his* father was a bilge rat who sailed on a pirate frigate called the *Queen Anne's Revenge* with a pleasant fellow named Black Beard. Heard of him, matey? Anyway, Serigala might be the wolf lord of this castle, but I'm the big rat of this Ouboo!" squealed Ratafia with pride. The other rats slinking in the corners hissed their approval and allegiance to Ratafia. One smaller rat who had been hiding in the corner to avoid the matchstick light crept up shyly behind Ratafia and squeak-hissed to get his attention.

"Arrr...what's boilin' inside yer head, Rat-a-Tat?" snarled Ratafia.

"Excuse me, Ratafia, sir. These pitiful tiny creatures that you call fluffy puffies are hamsters. Some humans keep them as pets." Rat-a-Tat was careful not to offend Ratafia.

"And what concern is that to me?" snarled Ratafia.

"Sir, I think they...are...rodents. And as you know, we are also—"

Rat-a-Tat was cut off briskly by Ratafia's sharp reply. "Rodents! I *know* we are rodents! What is your point?" asked Ratafia, who was a little annoyed by a lesser rat questioning his authority.

Rat-a-Tat continued, "Well, as you know, it is against your… code…to—"

"To eat other rodents? I am a rat! Not a filthy cannibal!" Ratafia was really annoyed now. "I've no hunger for fluffy puffies!" Ratafia squealed. He then turned back to Captain Nibbles.

"Avast ye, little puff. Come closer," Ratafia said to Captain Nibbles. "Light another one of yer fire sticks so I can see your tiny face in the light." Captain Nibbles inched closer to Ratafia and stopped right in front of him. He lit another match and held it under his face. The captain's head was almost as big as the big rat's nose.

Ratafia sniffed Captain Nibbles deeply, then spoke. "Hmm… you don't look like any rodent that I've ever laid eyes on. I've met squirrels, voles, and even Swedish Viking rats; but nothing that looks like you. So in truth, are you a rodent?" Ratafia had never seen a hamster before, and he seemed a tad perplexed.

"I am…we are. That is, we are rodents, sir," Captain Nibbles answered respectfully. Ratafia paused in thought, as if preparing to render his judgment. Then his big ratty mouth slowly curled into an awkward grin.

"Well then…welcome to Wolf Castle, me wee friends!" Ratafia announced to the hamsters. The rats along the wall all squeak-cheered, and all the hamsters breathed a deep sigh of relief. Their bones would not be gnawed on this day. Ratafia turned to the other rats and issued an order.

"We won't be plunderin' and pillagin' the Ouboo this day, mat-eys. And we won't be dining on these fluffy *hamsters*. I know yer all starvin'. Go, ya pie-rats! Plunder the pantry to yer hearts' content!" ordered Ratafia.

Instead of gnawing on the hamsters, the rats retreated through cracks in the castle walls, heading toward the castle galley to look for scraps of garbage. Ratafia stayed long enough to give Captain Nibbles and the other hamsters a warning about what awaited them.

"Avast, me hearties, tomorrow when the hot yellow ball in the sky rises to ruin our day, Nashoba will come to the dungeon to take you to see the big wolf, Serigala," warned Ratafia. "Be careful! He'll be very hamster hungry, but we'll be close by, hidin' and listenin' in the walls. When a bilge rat is what you need, a bilge rat will be there for ya." After he spoke, Ratafia disappeared through a shadowy crack in the ancient stone wall. Captain Nibbles doubted that he would ever see him again. Everyone knows you can't trust a rat.

Chapter 12

Castle Secrets

Castles have secret doors and hidden passageways. The rats would *almost* always escape the gnashing teeth of the hungry wolves because they knew every crack in every ancient wall. The rats and wolves hated each other, but they learned to live in the shadows together because they both loved the darkness. The rats preferred to live within the castle walls, despite the danger of the wolves' snapping teeth, because of the mountains of garbage that never seemed to run out. To a rat, this castle was a cold, damp, and gloomy paradise.

Ratafia caught up with his horde of rodent freebooters in the castle galley where the wolves' food was kept and prepared. They were busy gnawing on scraps of rancid meat and piles of rotting vegetables on the cold galley floor. Wolves are not fond of carrots, cabbages, and such; so vegetables were always left to fester and rot. As soon as Ratafia squeezed into the room through a jagged crack in the wall, all the rats sprang to attention, some with garbage hanging from their ratty lips.

"Get your bellies full up, ratties. We'll be headin' up to the Keep," Ratafia ordered. "We'll be waitin' in the walls tonight, but we won't be stayin' in the walls come first light. We might even come snout to snout with that son-of-a-biscuit eater Serigala! Respect the teeth of the wolf, me hearties, and sharpen yer own."

"But, Ratafia...sir," said an underling named Rattrap. "We've heard tell that Serigala can smell us inside the walls. Ain't it better for those *hamster* puffies to get chewed and swallowed rather than us?"

"They are family, Rattrap!" snapped Ratafia. "Tiny, puffy seed nibblers is all they are, but they are rodents just the same. Everyone's on deck in this battle! Enough of yer miserable mope whinin'. Now off with ya!"

One very large and overweight rat was still chewing on a rotten banana peel. He sputtered and choked as he tried to stuff even more of the peel into his sloppy wide mouth. Ratafia noticed his lack of attention and became agitated.

"Rattles, you miserable squeaker!" shouted Ratafia. "Have you even heard one word that's been comin' outa my bite hole?"

Rattles stopped chewing and looked up at Ratafia. Every rat was now staring directly at Rattles. The distracted rat tried to remember what Ratafia had just said. He started to panic but then shouted out the last thing he remembered, "You was sayin'...how we should all get our bellies full up!"

"Is that *all* you remember? Are you even with us, Rattles, or are you only here for the scraps n'booty?" asked Ratafia.

"May I finish my nibbles before I give you a proper answer, sir?" Rattles replied with stuffed cheeks.

"Avast, Rattles! My hope for ye to become a proper scoundrel is slippin' away," Ratafia snarled. The rest of the rats laughed and gathered around Ratafia to show him their support.

"Chew and swallow yer last bites, every last one of yas," Ratafia ordered. "We leave for the Keep in a quarter of a jiffer."

After eating so much that their bellies dragged on the cold castle floor, the rats followed Ratafia and squeezed through a scraggy crack in the wall and headed up to the Keep. When they arrived at the tower, they could hear Serigala's deep wolfish snores through the wall. They rested in the walls for the remainder of the night, digesting their food and waiting for the wolf king to awaken.

In the very early morning, Nashoba, the wolf captain of the guard, was summoned to the Keep to receive his orders from Serigala.

Nashoba entered the Keep, bowed down to the wolf king, and waited for his commands.

"Go to the oubliette and gather those tiny hamster pests and bring them so they can stand before me," ordered Serigala. "If any of them resist, Nashoba, feel free to enjoy a snack of your own." Nashoba left immediately with two other guard wolves to escort the hamsters from the lowest dungeon to the highest tower in the castle. When Nashoba arrived at the dungeon, the prisoners were just beginning to stir from their sleep. He looked down through the caged portal and into the darkness.

"Yoo-hoo, rise and shine, tiny jail rats," Nashoba said. "There is someone who wants to eat you, I mean, meet you." Nashoba giggle-growled at his own cleverness. He could hear the fear in the hamsters' voices.

"Is this the end of us, Captain Nibbles?" Corky asked in a shaky voice.

"I will never have the chance to live with humans. I'll never get to roll in a plastic ball. I'll never make children laugh!" lamented Rosie.

"I'll never be a true hero," groaned Wendell Cheeks. "Not if I end up in a wolf's belly. Heroes don't get eaten."

"I may have just enjoyed my last sleep and, worse yet, my last meal," bemoaned Two-Spots who was clearly still thinking about food. Nashoba lowered a knotted rope ladder down to the bottom of the damp cell.

"All right, hamster niblets, start climbing so I can introduce you to Serigala's empty stomach," Nashoba said with delight. "He might even let me have a taste just for delivering his breakfast." Captain Nibbles did his best to encourage his friends before they began their final climb.

"Hamsters! Remember your victories! You conquered the icy slop sink! You defeated the wild boars! You overcame the waterfall of death! You triumphed over the dark spirit of the Ouboo! Remember your victories and let your hearts rise up! Stop planning to die. Prepare your hearts to live!" Captain Nibbles's words were like a splash of cold water in the face.

"Prepare to live!" shouted Lola as she raised her needle sword.

"Prepare to live!" they all shouted. Captain Nibbles reached inside his pocket to feel the last two stones that were patiently waiting close to his heart.

Chapter 13

Night Songs

At Stumpy's Pet Shop, Barnaby was finishing his early morning rounds of cleaning nasty cages and feeding hungry bellies. On this particular morning, the animals were extremely restless and agitated. For some reason, there was an unusual amount of monkey chattering and poo tossing. The crested geckos barely ate their breakfast termites, and they didn't even touch last night's crickets. Barnaby grew suspicious when he noticed that the three cockatiel sisters were huddled together closer than usual. They were whispering secrets. He walked up to the java tree perch where the three sisters spent most of their time together.

"Good morning, ladies," Barnaby said calmly. "Are you having a pleasant sisterly conversation?"

After hearing the usual trills, whistles, and squawks, Cora Cockatiel, the eldest, answered politely, "Why yes, Master Barnaby. We were just dishin' the tea a bit. You know, a little babble and prattle among sisters, brawwwk. By the way, the seeds you gave us for brekky were absolutely delightful, absolutely delightful, brawwwk," Cora said nervously.

"I agree, Master Barnaby, brawwwk," said Camille Cockatiel. "The golden millet was simply to die for, to die for, brawk, brawwwk." Barnaby looked at them suspiciously. He doubted that they were discussing their delightful breakfast of golden millet, but what were they hiding? He looked at Candy, the youngest of the three cockatiels, and stared at her until she crumbled. He knew that if anyone would crack, it would be her. And crack she did. She broke like an old beaver dam during a hundred-year flood. She spoke so fast that it was difficult to hear all of her words.

"We all had the same dream last night, Master Barnaby, brawwwk! That's what we were jabberin' about. In our dream, there were dreadful wolves biting, filthy rats nipping, and hamsters with shiny daggers and arrows flying everywhere, flying everywhere! Brawwwk. There was howling, gnashing, and snarling. Gnashing and snarling, brawwwk." Cora and Camille were bobbing their heads in agreement.

"What else did you see, Candy?" urged Barnaby.

"Oh, Master Barnaby, we saw the sky split wide open, and three falcons darted down toward the earth. They were glittered with gold and had flaming feathers, flaming feathers, brawwwk. They circled the sky seven times, then one of them screamed, 'Come to us! Fight with us!' Brawwwk! What does it mean, Master Barnaby?"

"Those must be the castle falcons," said Barnaby. The falcons must have rebelled against Serigala since they granted you a vision. They're trying to help Captain Nibbles! Was there anything else? Try to remember, Candy!" urged Barnaby.

"The falcons were flying free, flying free, brawwk. No hoods, no leashes, brawwk. Once we were blind, but now we see, now we see, brawwwk," continued Candy.

"Don't forget the hamsters, brawwk," added Cora.

"What about the hamsters?" asked Barnaby.

Candy continued to share the dream. "I saw hamsters, many hamsters marching, marching, brawwwk. They were singing and marching, singing and marching, brawwwk. Lots of racket and clamor, racket and clamor, brawwwk! Then we all woke up and shared the same dream, the same dream, brawwwk! What does it mean, Master Barnaby? Brawwwkk." Barnaby looked at all three of the cockatiel sisters, who were shaking and moving nervously on their perch.

"It was not a dream you had, but a night song," said Barnaby.

"A night song?" asked Cora. "Brawwwkk."

"Yes, a night song…a vision," answered Barnaby. "The falcons were giving you a vision. It was a cry for help." Barnaby paused in thought, then spoke softly to himself. "I know what I must do."

Barnaby stood in the middle of the pet shop, stepped up on a rickety old packing crate, and cleared his voice.

"Everyone gather close and listen carefully. I've been called to help Captain Nibbles in his darkest hour. My heart breaks to tell you that I must leave Stumpy's Pet Shop immediately. Captain Nibbles needs me now, more than ever. It might already be too late, but I must try." He looked around to see tears welling up in the eyes of his precious pet friends. The rabbits and hedgehogs were trying to hold back tears, and some of the monkeys were inconsolable. Their weeping was loud and relentless. Even Ignacio the Iguana blinked furiously, fighting back tears that began to flood his eyes. To hide his emotions, he blamed it on his allergies, trying to convince anyone who would listen. But none of the other animals tried to hide their sadness. They could not imagine what life would be like without Barnaby's loving care.

"Wipe your eyes, lads and lassies!" exclaimed Barnaby. "There *is* good news! I have *three* choices to offer you," he said as many of the animals choked back tears. "You can stay here, at the pet shop, and let Ichabod Stump take care of you, or I can set you free. You can take your chances and live out your lives in the forest."

"Some choices!" an albino ferret quickly yelled out. "We either live out our lives being mistreated by that animal hater, Ichabod, or we wander through the brush and get eaten by a fox, a wolverine, or a bear." Ferrets can often be quite hasty in speaking their minds too quickly. Many of the animals agreed with the pessimistic ferret and began to growl and grumble.

"Wait," said a shy baby angora rabbit. She was so small and timid that her voice could hardly be heard. "Mr. Barnaby said we have *three* choices. But he has only shared two choices with us. What is our third choice, Mr. Barnaby, sir?" The pet shop animals felt embarrassed and slightly admonished by such a young and tiny rabbit. All the animals grew quiet and still, waiting for Barnaby's answer.

"Your third choice…is to come with *me* to the castle," said Barnaby invitingly. "Now, I am going to do something that you might not understand. I am going to unlock your cages and open your doors. Whatever you decide will be a giant step of faith, but it will be your choice alone." He walked about the pet shop, unlocking each cage. It was agonizing for Barnaby to give the animals in his care a free choice to follow him or walk away from him. Oh, how his heart would be broken if they didn't step out of their cages. Oh, how his soul would be crushed if he saw them scurry away to live alone in the forest without him. But he knew in his heart that they all had to choose of their own free will.

An astonishing thing happened when Barnaby finished unlocking all the cages. The monkeys shyly stepped out of their cages first. Next, the lemurs timidly exited their confines. Rabbits hopped slowly out of their hutches, sniffed the air, then stopped. Not one of the animals in the pet shop flew, hopped, darted, or slithered away. They all stared at Barnaby like soldiers waiting for their marching orders. Soon, all the animals were out of their cages. The spotted turtles and the pond sliders took a little longer, naturally, but they too were finally free of their enclosures. Barnaby's heart danced inside him as he witnessed the decision they made for themselves and for him. He paused for a moment, for his very breath had left him. After wiping the tears from his cheeks, he spoke.

"This is a wonderful, magnificent day! We leave for the basket fort immediately!"

"Wonderful day, magnificent day, brawwwk," declared Cora Cockatiel.

"I have a very strong feeling that Chadwick the Holy received the same night song. He will be waiting for us," said Barnaby as he turned his face toward Fort Chewy. He began his march with hundreds of pet shop animals closely behind him.

Chapter 14

Feather from the Sky

The next day at the basket fort, the hamsters were out and about, busy about many things. Buttercup and Eye Patch were gathering seeds and berries. Puff Bottom and Mr. Whiskers were out searching for new hidden springs of water, but still having no luck. Fudge Bar, Freckles, Corn Chip, and Cletus were engaged in a fun and exhilarating contest of jousting, using baby carrots, even though they were told not to play with their food. Einstein was very focused, using a stick to write out complex mathematical formulas in the dirt. Giggles and Cheerio were sitting on a tree stump laughing at Jiggety Jumper who was trying to juggle slippery cherry pits. Julian Bouchard, the French stowaway hamster, was holding an outdoor class, not only teaching younger hamsters the musical French language, but also reading from an adapted version of *A Tale of Two Cities*. The whole hamster camp bustled about, while still waiting for a sign that Captain Nibbles and their company of brothers had survived their perilous journey. Chadwick the Holy was resting on a rock under a sweet large gum tree, meditating on the night song he had received in a dream the night before. He hadn't told the rest of the hamsters about the vision yet. He feared that the hamsters in the fort would die of fright if he told them about snapping, snarling wolves. The cockatiel sisters received the same vision at the pet shop.

Eye Patch was the first one to look up and see the magnificent birds soaring above the camp.

"Falcons!" shouted Eye Patch. He alerted the whole fort, and everyone froze as they looked to the sky, fearful of an attack. There is nothing more terrifying to a hamster than a circling falcon right above its head.

"Wait!" exclaimed Einstein. "They are not attacking. Look, they are descending in a slow, drifting spiral. They are coming in peace." All the hamsters gathered to witness the descent of the majestic birds. Chadwick the Holy came out from under the shade of the sweet gum tree to join the others. They all looked up in guarded anticipation.

"Be careful. It might be a trick," squeaked Buttercup with a warning.

"It is not a trick," answered Chadwick the Holy. "I remember the words from the *Songs of Light*. We sang them as hamster pups. 'Hope will come on golden wings, drifting down like a feather from the sky.'" The falcons drifted lower and lower in a lazy downward spiral. The two beautiful peregrine falcons followed the lead of a very large and majestic gyrfalcon. The hamsters stood motionless as they gazed with wonder at the remarkable birds. The falcons' gentle sky dance continued until they landed gracefully in front of the waiting hamsters. Chadwick the Holy and Einstein stepped cautiously toward the birds, with dozens of hamsters behind them.

"Welcome, sky messengers," Chadwick addressed them with respect.

"It is an honor…to have you…in our camp," Einstein said warily.

"We're so happy that you didn't come here to eat us," said Corn Chip plainly.

"Quiet, Corn Chip," Chadwick said in a hushed tone. "They might change their minds." The assembled hamsters looked up in awe at the massive bird with golden wings. They waited silently for the gyrfalcon to speak.

"We no longer serve the wolf king," said the gyrfalcon. "Rufus, our falconer, is an old and forgetful wolf. He often forgets to secure our falcon hoods. From our perch, we could see for the first time how evil the wolves were becoming. We saw Nashoba leading Captain Nibbles and his friends across the courtyard toward the oubliette. As they walked, the captain looked up, and our eyes met. In an instant, something profound happened. I could see goodness and light flowing from him. At the same time, I could feel the weight of evil when I saw how savage and bloodthirsty the wolves were behaving in the courtyard. Every time Serigala's name was chanted by the castle wolves, my stomach turned. I realized that *we* were being held captive as well. We were being used to help him grow stronger and even more evil," explained the gyrfalcon.

"How did you break away from the castle?" asked Chadwick the Holy.

"Our legs were still bound to the ironwood perch by leather leashes. We knew if we were to help Captain Nibbles, we would have to fly free, so we snapped the leather straps with our powerful and sharp beaks," said the gyrfalcon. Einstein wanted to ask questions but decided not to interrupt the massive bird when he saw the size of his curled talons. The gyrfalcon continued, "We flew off into the forest and rested on the branch of a dragon blood tree. I fell into the deepest of sleeps and dreamed of the hamsters and their vicious battle with the wolves. In a vision, I saw hamsters from your basket fort, moving toward Wolf Castle to help Captain Nibbles. At the same time, I dreamed of the three cockatiel sisters, Barnaby, and hundreds of his animal friends joining them from the pet shop. Somehow my night song drifted to the sleeping sisters at the pet store and to Chadwick the Holy at the basket fort."

"Uh, wait *just* a minute… *We're* the hamster army?" asked Corn Chip.

"We only pretend fight… We only attack each other…with baby carrots," Giggles said, trying to hide a giggle. Now that he said it out loud it, it really did seem silly. Buttercup and Mr. Whiskers couldn't believe what they were hearing.

"Look at us! We're tiny rodents, not lions or wolverines!" Buttercup shouted.

"We're *just* hamsters! A quick swipe of a gopher's paw would knock us clean into next week!" yelled Mr. Whiskers. "Pow! Right into next week!"

Chadwick the Holy stepped forward to address the hamsters. "Where has your faith flown off to, young hamsters? Barnaby saw something remarkable in you. You need to see yourselves the way he sees you. You're not just mindless wheel runners or tiny pocket pets. You see yourselves as happy little balls of fur; but you *are* a majestic army, chosen to be fearless in times of peril, and charged with bringing hope to the hopeless." After Chadwick had spoken, the gyrfalcon raised one magnificent wing, pointing toward a movement on the path.

"For those who still don't believe, look!" cried the falcon. All the hamsters of Fort Chewy turned to see a smiling Barnaby, marching from Stumpy's Pet Shop with hundreds of animals close behind him. There were rainbow lorikeets on Barnaby's shoulders and finger monkeys peeking their tiny heads out of his jacket pockets. Otters playfully scrambled behind him, and brightly colored parrots flew from tree to tree. Hope was renewed in the fifty-four hamsters at the sight of Barnaby and his broad smile. Their hearts exploded with thanksgiving as they remembered how Barnaby had saved them from a pirate's funeral and gave them a second chance to live. As Barnaby approached them, there was a great reunion with weeping and hugs and joyful celebration.

When the excitement lessened, the great falcon opened his golden wings, and everyone grew quiet. Barnaby stood next to Chadwick the Holy, representing the joining of the pet store animals and the hamsters from Fort Chewy. There was only one more reunion to complete this holy trinity. Joining with Captain Nibbles and his company of brave hearts would give them full strength against the castle wolves. The cord of three strands would soon be completed and would not be easily broken.

"It is time to fulfill your destinies!" thundered the mighty gyrfalcon. "Come with us to the castle and witness a new dawn!" He and the two majestic peregrines opened their wings and flew back toward Wolf Castle. They all watched the falcons fly away. Barnaby encouraged all the animals from the pet shop and all the hamsters from Fort Chewy to set their faces firmly toward the castle.

"'Tis time to fill up your hearts with courage and thanksgiving," said Barnaby. "Captain Nibbles needs us."

Chapter 15

The Wolf King

Inside the castle of the wolves, Nashoba led the captive hamsters up a dark ancient stairwell. Upward they went, higher and higher, until they reached the pinnacle of the castle. Once they reached the top, they were led down a cold, lonely hallway to Serigala's quarters. Standing at the closed entrance to his quarters, the hamsters marveled at the great oak doors, then shivered knowing that Serigala was just on the other side. The massive oak doors were three inches thick with two heavy iron door knockers, each depicting the head of an angry, snarling wolf. A three-foot knotted rope hung from each iron ring. Nashoba stood on his hind legs and took the knotted rope in his teeth. He slammed the thick, heavy circle against the door three times, creating an echo that made the hamsters' tiny bodies shudder. Both doors began to open slowly from the inside. Two guard wolves strained with ropes in their sharp teeth to pull open the heavy doors and reveal a most terrifying sight. There stood Serigala, basking in his own magnificence and splendor. He was twice the size of any of the other castle wolves, and his fur was blacker than a tempest cloud. His eyes were flaming amber, and his stare captured the souls of every hamster. The lips of the wolf king were curled back into a cruel and vicious grin, revealing the largest and sharpest teeth they had ever seen.

"Enter, tiny hamster warriors. Don't be shy. You are just in time…for breakfast," invited Serigala. They could feel the heaviness of evil in the wolf's voice. After the *invitation* was given to enter, Nashoba escorted the hamsters deeper into the dark medieval room. The galley steward was present and waiting to find out what Serigala desired for his first meal of the day. The steward waited in the shadows as the wolf king addressed the hamsters.

"I see that you are all carrying weapons?" inquired Serigala. "How delightful! They are so tiny...and charming. I just love the wee bows and arrows and precious little daggers. I think I might lie down and die of fright as we speak," Serigala said with a heavy measure of sarcasm. "I told the wolf guards not to take your weapons away from you. They seem rather harmless, and they look so adorable."

Captain Nibbles remained calm and patient as Serigala continued to mock the hamsters. Chewy, Two-Spots, and Corky began to feel less fearful and more agitated each time Serigala spoke. Toby gripped his bow tightly. They felt their warrior spirits rising inside them. They patiently continued to listen to the wolf king.

"I have called you to my chambers for two reasons," continued the great wolf. "First, you must know that you will never prevail against the kingdom of wolves. We rule this castle and the forest beyond as far as the eye can see. You have read the *Songs of Light*, I gather? I read it every day. I know it far better than you. Everything in it is a lie, a trash pile of false hopes and vain imaginations." Serigala paused to express a deep sigh and growl before continuing. "It says in your *book of nonsense* that the meek shall inherit the earth. Look around and behold the power and terror of the wolf. Do we look meek to you? The meek will inherit nothing!" Serigala's voice was thunderous.

Lola squeezed the handle of her dagger tightly as Serigala continued his mockeries. Ratafia and his band of rats were listening from within the stone walls. They listened and waited.

"Now, the second reason that I called you to my chambers, to be honest, is that I am famished," said Serigala as if he were getting bored. "Now, enough talking. I am quite ready for breakfast," said Serigala. He looked over his choices for breakfast. Looking down the line of hamsters standing before him, Two-Spots caught his eye immediately. What he saw was a very plump hamster with a belly that hung rather proudly over his dagger belt. Two-Spots made Serigala's mouth water immediately because he was quite larger and meatier than the others. The galley steward stepped forward to take the wolf king's breakfast order. The other wolves in the castle always waited patiently for Serigala to finish his breakfast before they ate because the alpha always ate first. Serigala was always slow to finish his breakfast, just to remind the other wolves of their order and place in the castle.

"Steward, I would like this hamster turned slowly on the spit," Serigala ordered as he pointed to Two-Spots. "Tell the spit master to turn him slowly, very slowly."

"Will that be all, Your Magnificence?" asked the steward, who was a small and older wolf.

"Have the plump hamster served with a side order of castle rats, if you can catch a few," answered Serigala.

The hamsters' grip on their daggers and bows grew stronger, and their focus intensified. The guard wolves stepped forward to take Two-Spots to the galley to be prepared for the wolf king's breakfast.

As they took hold of his tiny arms, Captain Nibbles stepped forward and yelled out without much thought, "Wait! You do not want to eat this one." He pointed to Two-Spots. "He may look tasty, but he is a rather disgusting chap in every respect. I fear he would incite bedlam in your bowels and cause you severe gastric pandemonium."

"Who are you, and what words are spouting from your impudent squeak hole?" asked Serigala.

The galley steward attempted to interpret Captain Nibbles's words. "He is saying, Your Highness, if you eat this hamster, you will most likely become…gassy," said the steward carefully.

"I am Captain Nathaniel Nibbles, sir, and we are the lost hamsters of Barnaby Bunch," the captain said proudly.

"Then if you are lost, Barnaby Bunch must be looking for you, Mr. Nibbles," replied Serigala. "Oh, what fun! I think it's going to be a grand party here at the old castle. So what is your suggestion, you nervy little squeaker with wee dotty eyes? If I don't eat this fat, spongy hamster, whom do you suggest I have for my first meal?"

"Eat me, sir. I believe that I would more than satisfy your first meal needs," Captain Nibbles said confidently. The captain felt noble in offering himself in place of Two-Spots.

Serigala paused for a moment, then spoke to the galley steward. "I have changed my mind, steward," said the wolf king. "I have decided…that I will have *all* these pathetic tiny beasts for my breakfast. Put a skewer through them all and roast them on the spit. Tell the spit master to turn them quickly. I am starving. I don't mind if they are a little raw at the center. Take them and prepare them now. Get them out of my sight!" Serigala's lips curled tighter, flashing his knifelike teeth. The coarse hair on his thick muscular neck stood up, and his heavy claws tapped the stone castle floor. He was growing increasingly impatient and hungry.

Captain Nibbles realized that his plan to save Two-Spots had failed miserably because it was not completely thought out from beginning to end. He had now put *all* the hamsters in severe peril. As he stood next to Chewy, he leaned closer to him.

"I am so sorry, Chewy. I have let all of you down. I fear that this may truly be the end of our journey together. It has been an honor to lead you," Captain Nibbles whispered with deep remorse.

"You are not giving up now, are you, Captain? You told us to prepare to live. You told us to remember all the things we have conquered. You told us to remember the stones!" urged Chewy.

"I have but two stones left, the water stone and the light stone," answered Captain Nibbles. "I have to be wise in knowing when to use them. Barnaby told me to *only* use them when necessary. He said—"

"Captain! Snap out of it! We're about to be served on a breakfast platter!" Chewy screamed. "Barnaby gave you the five stones in his absence. Even though the sun is shining brightly outside, it's dark in here, Captain. It's *really* dark! It has *never* been darker! We need the light stone right now, Captain!" Chewy pleaded. "Use the stone, Captain! Use it, *now*!"

Chapter 16

Rats in the Walls

The guard wolves crept toward the hamsters to lead them to the galley where they would be prepared for breakfast. Captain Nibbles quickly reached for his dagger, as did the other hamsters. Chewy, Two-Spots, Corky, and Toby readied their bows and quickly reached behind to grab an arrow from their quivers. The hamsters moved to make a defensive circle. The archers aimed their arrows, and the others held daggers tightly in their fists. After the wolves laughed at the hamsters' display of bravery and tiny weapons, they bared their teeth and let out a monstrous howl as they moved closer to the ring of tiny rodents. Captain Nibbles opened his hand to reveal the white light stone. When the hamsters saw its brilliance, their hearts were strengthened. The captain issued a firm and final command.

"Shield your eyes, hamster warriors!" the captain yelled. The hamsters covered their eyes, then with a loud cry, Captain Nibbles threw the white stone with all his strength against the castle floor. A flash of pure white light surged from the stone and stunned Serigala and Nashoba with momentary blindness. Darkness completely overwhelmed them and took away their eyesight. Suddenly, a war cry was heard from *within* the stone walls. Serigala and Nashoba, blinded by the light, turned to hear the incoming rats screaming, "Urrah!" a battle cry mixed with terrifying squeaks and squeals. Ratafia and scores of rats poured into the tower room through cracks in the wall. Captain Nibbles and the other hamsters shouted back, "Ha-ooh!" as they witnessed reinforcements streaming from the cold castle walls to help them in their darkest hour. The guard wolves were stunned and confused as the rats attacked from all sides of the room as the captain was ordering the hamster archers to take aim. The daggers and arrows were not deadly, but very painful as they found their marks in the paws and hindquarters of the enemy. Wolves were hopping, howling, barking, and bellowing. The rats were jumping on the backs of all the wolves, including Nashoba and Serigala. The shrieks and squeals of the rats were ear piercing as they continued their assault on the wolves. Lola and Rosie were clinging to Nashoba's tail, jabbing it over and over with their tiny needle daggers. The guard wolves were howling in retreat to escape the piercing attack. Soon they left the tower Keep completely, leaving Nashoba and Serigala to defend themselves. The rats continued their attack against the wolves with nips, bites, and scratchy swipes of their paws, while screeching, "Rat bite fever, urrah!" The attack was a sudden and furious storm that rained down relentless pain. Serigala was spinning in circles blindly, trying to bite Ratafia who was hanging on to his massive tail. The two wolves were gnashing their teeth and snapping their jaws, hoping to find any rat or hamster they could sink their teeth into. However, the hamsters and rats were too fast and cunning for the wolves as they continued their attack.

While the battle was escalating within Serigala's Keep, the wolves in the watchtower were sounding the alarm of another attack. The wolves inside the castle dashed about in frantic disarray, realizing that they were being attacked from *within* and from *without* the castle walls. They looked beyond the walls and saw Barnaby Bunch marching toward the castle with hundreds of his pet store animal friends and fifty-four very brave hamsters from Fort Chewy. When Barnaby reached the edge of the moat, he realized that there was no way to cross into the castle with the drawbridge up. He had to enter the castle to help Captain Nibbles but seemed to be at a dead end. He was desperately trying to find a way to cross the moat, when he heard a frantic squeaking. Barnaby turned to see a very portly rodent jumping up and down and waving his tiny ratty hands.

THE LOST HAMSTERS OF BARNABY BUNCH

"Over here, sir! Come quickly!" yelled Rattles, the portly rat. Barnaby quickly moved toward the rotund rodent, with hundreds of animals following him.

"Friend or foe, Rat?" questioned Barnaby.

"Avast, I'm here to shuttle you safely inside the castle, sir. Me ratties are helping our hamster brothers inside. There's no time to lose!" shouted Rattles. "Ratafia says I just might earn me stripes if I lead you safely inside the castle walls. There be a secret passage that leads under the moat into the courtyard! Follow me, but hurry, we must!"

Barnaby had never trusted a rat before, but this was as good a time as any to start. Rattles scampered along the bank of the moat with Barnaby and his followers closely behind. The very round rat came to a wooden trapdoor in the ground, covered by quack grass and knapweed. Rattles motioned for Barnaby to lift the door by its crude metal handle. After he flung the wooden door open, he looked down inside to see a steep rickety stairwell leading down into the darkness.

"The passage goes *under* the moat, sir. Take the first steps down, walk under the moat, then up a second set of stairs. You'll be comin' out inside the castle. You'll find yourself in the middle of the courtyard, ya will, but probably not to cheers and applause," squeaked Rattles.

"I've never trusted a castle rat before," exclaimed Barnaby.

"Well, I've never trusted a scary man-beast either, so I guess we'll be countin' it even," answered Rattles.

"You have certainly earned your stripes, dear Rat. Thank you!" Barnaby replied.

"Just put in a good word for me when you meet the big rat, Ratafia. Go, now!" Rattles squeaked loudly, then left Barnaby to join his rat brothers in the fight again.

Barnaby and his pet shop friends filed *down* the uneven wooden steps and slogged through the damp passageway under the moat until it came to another set of steps. As they climbed up the steps, Barnaby slowly pushed up on a wooden door. Sunlight streamed into the tunnel. Just as Rattles had told him, he was now looking at the large courtyard *inside* the castle. There was already chaos everywhere, but the wolves panicked even more when they saw an old man and hundreds of animals entering the castle courtyard. The two guard wolves were overwrought with fear as they ran aimlessly through the castle, alerting the other wolves.

"Run for your lives!" they yowled. "Every wolf for himself!" they howled.

Every wolf fled the castle through the closest escape passage. They fled the castle and ran off into the forest in every direction, shaken to their core. The guard wolves did not have time in the confusion to tell the other wolves that the attackers were only one old man, some pet store animals, and a band of tiny squealing hamsters. Barnaby's invaders had no weapons; only a determination to fight evil. The two tower guards fled the castle as well, howling as they disappeared into the thick cover of the forest. Barnaby and his friends now had control of the courtyard, with the golden falcons swooping down to chase the remaining wolves from the castle and into the dark forest. The battle continued in Serigala's Keep.

"Banzai!" yelled Captain Nibbles, as the rat and hamster warriors continued their skirmish with the wolves. Nashoba was covered with nipping rats while being poked by daggers in his paws and having arrows find their mark on the tip of his cold black nose. He finally let out a monstrous howl, running toward the thick oak doors to make his escape from the room. Rats jumped off as they watched Nashoba retreat and flee in agony. The frightened wolf fled down the stone castle steps and through the open courtyard, as Barnaby and his pet companions cheered. Nashoba made his escape through the same passageway that brought Barnaby into the castle. He ran down the steps, under the putrid moat, then up the steps and into the dark forest. Serigala was now the only wolf left in the castle. He tried to howl for help, but he sounded more like a very sick goose. There was a pause in the battle as Serigala realized that he was the only wolf left in the fight. His wide chest heaved from exhaustion, and his legs were weak and trembling. The rats and hamsters formed a circle around Serigala. All eyes were looking up at the tired, defeated wolf. Serigala crouched down on the castle floor, resting his head on his front paws. He was ready to accept defeat, at least for now. Captain

Nibbles stepped forward with his dagger still drawn just in case it was a trick. The big wolf bowed down, surrendering to Captain Nibbles and Ratafia. As soon as Serigala surrendered, there arose a thunderous cheer from both the hamster warriors and Ratafia's band of rodent hearties.

The tiny hamster Two-Spots found himself standing side by side with Rattles, the large portly rat. Two-Spots was breathing hard and turned to Rattles, who was huffing and puffing from the battle. They looked at each other's puffy bellies and felt a kindred spirit.

"I don't know about you, but all of this fighting has given me a sad, empty belly," Two-Spots confessed as he looked up at the much larger and fatter rodent.

"We must be brothers from another rodent mother," Rattles answered as he looked down at the tiny warrior. "My noggin's been in a fog just thinkin' about a brawny snack for half the battle. I've been feeling right hollow since the tussle started," Rattles continued.

"So perhaps a snack and a snooze when we're all through here?" countered Two-Spots.

"Avast, just so it ain't bunny grub. I need somethin' more hearty, like cod stew and cackle fruit with gobs of black pepper," countered Rattles.

"Not sure what those things are," answered Two-Spots, "but we'll find *something* that will satisfy our bellies."

The hamster archers, with bows and arrows at the ready, along with Ratafia's army of rats, escorted Serigala through the wolf-empty castle to the open courtyard. Captain Nibbles immediately gazed upon the most wonderful sight anyone could have imagined. There stood Barnaby and his legion of pet shop friends, sharing in the victory. He then saw Chadwick the Holy standing proudly with the other hamsters from Fort Chewy. There was a tremendous display of emotion.

"What is happening to me, Ratafia?" cried Rattles. "My face is wet! I think it's leaking!"

"Avast, you bumblehead! Those are tears," answered Ratafia. "But it sure is a wretched, ugly look on you." Ratafia laughed. Rattles tried to wipe his face roughly with two chubby rat paws.

"I can't help it," cried Rattles. "It's such a beautiful thing. Look at all the love bein' dished out." Rattles tried to keep his crying to a whimper. "Maybe…a nice Banbury cake…would comfort me," sniveled Rattles. The whole stone courtyard was splash-dotted with big drops of joyful tears.

Serigala watched the display of affection with disgust. He knew that this might be his only chance to escape. While the hamsters were distracted with joyful celebration, Serigala slowly inched backward. He was slowly regaining his eyesight as he broke toward an escape passage near the wall. It was hidden behind empty, turned-over water barrels. In a flash, Serigala disappeared through a secret passage in the stone wall and vanished under the moat and into the thick cover of the forest. He wandered aimlessly, limping and growling under his breath. His wolf army had completely abandoned him. Serigala was now a lone wolf without any followers in the world. The animals of the forest would never again fear this sad and defeated wolf.

As Serigala staggered and hobbled through the brush, he came upon a chipmunk named Blinky Nutmuffin. The chipmunk crouched on a rotting log just staring curiously at the battered wolf. Normally a chipmunk would skitter away in terror at the sight of a wolf, but Blinky sat staring at the battered beast. Serigala looked at the curious chipmunk and tried his best to growl but was only able to muster a weak and pathetic yowl. Blinky stared back at him, then broke into a chittering chuckle.

"You dare laugh at the *great* Serigala?" the giant wolf asked indignantly.

"*Great?* Everyone in the forest knows that you were skunked and outsmarted by a band of my scruffy rodent cousins," chittered Blinky. "We've all seen your wolves dashing through the forest like chickens in a thunderstorm."

"Well, I will have the very last laugh, you sassy garden rat," promised Serigala.

"Of course you will," countered Blinky sarcastically. "So are you planning to retake the castle all by yourself?"

"That's none of your concern, chipmunk!" Serigala said angrily. "But I promise you this. The hamsters' reign in the castle will be short-lived. Before we fled the castle, I ordered my wolf servants to knock over the water barrels and to pollute the castle well. My wolves poisoned the only source of drinking water that they have. The well is poisoned, the moat is polluted, and their water supply is empty. Thirst will do them in by week's end," he said with an evil laugh. Serigala found great joy at the thought that Captain Nibbles and all the castle trespassers would be suffering soon.

"You are a very vile and wicked wolf, Serigala," uttered Blinky Nutmuffin.

"Thank you, I know," replied Serigala with an evil grin.

The battered wolf limped away and curled up to rest under the shade of an ugly and poisonous sandbox tree. After licking his wounds, he dozed off to a very disturbed sleep, dreaming about the annihilation of all hamsters and retaking the castle. Blinky knew he had to make it to the castle quickly to warn Captain Nibbles and the other animals before they drank from the poisoned waters.

Chapter 17

Eau de Vie

Blinky Nutmuffin reached the castle out of breath. The drawbridge was up, so he had no way of crossing into the castle to warn those inside. He could smell the stench of the moat water and couldn't help wondering if he was too late. Did the hamsters and other animals already drink the poisoned waters from the castle well?

After he caught his breath, Blinky chittered and chattered as loud as he could, trying to get the attention of anyone in the castle who could hear him. Minutes went by, and two emperor penguins appeared over the castle wall. The two penguin tower guards, Mr. Beaks and J. W. Waddleman, looked at each other, wondering what to do. They looked down at the tiny striped rodent who was standing on the other side of the moat. They were often on tower watch but had never encountered a hysterical chipmunk before.

"The water! Don't drink!" screamed Blinky from across the moat. The two penguins were very confused and looked at each other with blank stares.

"What did he say?" said Mr. Beaks, leaning over the wall to try to hear the chipmunk.

"I think he said...*the otter...don't stink*," Waddleman answered, taking a guess.

"It doesn't make *any* sense," Mr. Beaks replied.

"It might make sense to otters," answered Waddleman. "*They* might be happy to know that they don't stink."

Mr. Beaks rolled his eyes, then yelled to Blinky to be clearer, "What otter don't stink?"

"No! Not otter! The water...don't drink! It's poisoned!" screamed Blinky Nutmuffin. When the penguins heard and finally understood Blinky's frantic words, they immediately ordered the lowering of the massive drawbridge to let him cross. As soon as the bridge came down and the castle was opened before him, the chipmunk scampered across the wooden bridge and into the courtyard of the castle. Once inside, Blinky Nutmuffin jumped up and down and waved his tiny arms, screaming and screeching to anyone who would listen.

"The water is poisoned! Don't...drink...the...water!"

Everyone who had been sleeping began to pour into the courtyard, including Captain Nibbles and Barnaby Bunch. Soon the entire castle was awake, all because of a screeching, chattering chipmunk who was getting hoarse trying to warn everyone.

"Who are you, and where do you come from, young chipmunk?" asked Captain Nibbles.

"I'm Blinky Nutmuffin, sir. I live in the forest near the dewberry grove," answered Blinky. "I've come here to warn you, sir."

"Warn us?" inquired Barnaby. "Warn us of what?"

"Has anyone here taken a drink from the courtyard well?" asked Blinky.

"A few have tried, but they said there was a foul stench in the water. We've been existing on the meager supply that we brought with us on our journey," said Barnaby, "but we know it won't last much longer."

"What is your concern, Nutmuffin? What do *you* know about the castle water?" Captain Nibbles questioned.

"It's been poisoned by the wolves! Serigala told me himself last night. I met him in the forest. He looked like someone had beaten him with a hickory stick, but he kept moanin' and groanin' about how he was going to get even. Then he started laughin' about how he poisoned the water in the castle. He said that he would come back to the castle when everyone there went belly-up from drinking the poison," warned the chipmunk.

"Set guards around the well! No one is to drink from it!" shouted Captain Nibbles.

"You shall no longer be called Blinky Nutmuffin," declared Barnaby. "From this day forward, you shall be called Sir Blinky the Brave. Your small voice and big heart may have just saved our lives."

The lack of water was already beginning to show in the faces of the animals. The birds were warbling incoherently. The sloths, who were usually slow-moving, were not moving at all. They were frozen statues stuck to the sides of trees. The playful capuchins looked snoozy and dazed. Even the turtles were moving slower than the garden snails. The entire castle was bone-dry. Barnaby's throat was dry, and his lips were blistered from lack of water. Even he was tempted to drink from the well, even though he knew it was foul and deadly. Barnaby began to cough and wheeze.

"We're down to our last few drops of good water, Captain," cautioned Chadwick the Holy. "How are we going to survive? We'll only make it a few days without a drink."

Barnaby's face was ashen, and his knees were wobbly. Captain Nibbles looked at every precious life in the castle and could see that everyone was desperate for fresh water to survive. He knew that the moat was befouled and undrinkable. He also knew that the wolves had dumped over the water barrels when they were escaping, probably ordered by Serigala. Hope seemed to be disappearing in the castle, but Captain Nibbles refused to give up as he called everyone to gather closer. He raised his voice as loud as he could.

"Wasn't the flame stone used to help us defeat Sir Walter Fat Belly at his campsite?" the captain began. "And didn't the life stone bring Wendell Cheeks back from the swallowing waterfall? And when the oubliette tried to erase us and make us disappear so that we would be forgotten, wasn't it the hope stone that let us be seen again! And finally, didn't the light stone blind the wolves during our battle so that we could retake the castle?"

"We haven't forgotten," answered Chewy. "But we are dying of thirst. And if this is the end of us, those other stones don't really matter, do they?"

"Unless…there is one more stone," said Barnaby knowingly, with a cracked voice.

"*Is* there one more stone, Captain?" asked Chewy.

Captain Nibbles raised his fist into the air, holding the water stone tightly in his grasp. "One more stone!" Captain Nibbles shouted. With the stone held tightly in his fist, Captain Nibbles whistled a command for the appearance of the golden gyrfalcon.

In mere seconds, the magnificent gyrfalcon swept down out of the bright blue sky. He landed delicately in front of Captain Nibbles and bowed his head to the ground. The beautiful castle falcon was humbled because he seemed to already know why he was being summoned. The captain climbed upon the falcon's back and took a tight hold of his neck feathers. As everyone in the castle watched, the falcon's beautiful golden wings were opened wide. He lifted up into the cloudless blue sky with Captain Nibbles on his back. As the gyrfalcon circled high above the earth, everyone who was gathered in the courtyard looked up to witness a miracle. Suddenly, the mighty falcon dove back down toward the earth like an arrow. Captain Nibbles held on to the falcon's neck feathers with one hand, and with the other hand, he held the blue water stone high above his head. They descended like a bolt of lightning. Just as they came closer to the earth, Captain Nibbles threw the stone downward with all his might. The stone found its target and struck a small clearing in the courtyard. There was a terrific explosion of blinding light and color as the stone struck the ground. The earth began to tremble just before it split the dry ground wide open. An incredible gush of fresh spring water exploded out of the earth, spraying and soaking everyone and everything in the courtyard. The hamsters and the rats began to fill bucket after bucket of the sweet spring water that jetted out of the new opening in the ground. Joyful laughter filled the courtyard. Monkeys made mudslides. Parrots sat on perches with their heads tilted back and their beaks wide open, collecting long, cool drinks.

"Eau de Vie! Sweet water of life!" shouted Cora, the cockatiel. Otters were lying on their backs spitting fountains of water into the air. Twin baby elephants stomped through deep puddles, then used their trunks to spray everyone in sight.

"Truly a spring of providence!" shouted Barnaby. After Captain Nibbles and the gyrfalcon landed back in the courtyard, all the animals could be seen refreshing themselves with long gulps from the sweet, fresh spring water. A team of beavers immediately began to build an aqueduct leading from the spring to the moat. Later, they would build an aqueduct from the moat to the streams and ponds in the forest down below. The just and the unjust would be refreshed by the Eau de Vie.

Barnaby ordered a stone memorial to be built around the open spring and proclaimed that it should forever be called Providence Spring. Fresh bubbling water still flows from Providence Spring to this day. Everyone who drinks from it is filled with joyful vitality.

Everyone celebrated until the sun changed into a reddish orange candy, melting and dripping over the horizon. Soon the blackness of the sky covered the earth and gave birth to millions of stars. As the hours went by and the animals tired of passionate feasting and gleeful jubilation, they all fell into a deep sleep with smiles on their faces and joy in their hearts. It wasn't long before peaceful sleep came to the animals, even the rats and the falcons. The falcons perched wherever they desired, not being tethered to a perch or being blinded by a hooded veil. And the rats slept freely in the open, instead of hiding in the cold dark walls of the castle. Captain Nibbles remained awake. He watched over the courtyard where hundreds of animals were sleeping peacefully under the soft light of brilliant stars. He soon grew tired and found a quiet corner in one of the towers to curl up and rest for the night. He slowly drifted off to the steady sound of monkey snores and the rhythmic nose whistling of Two-Spots.

Just before Captain Nibbles fell into a deep sleep, he heard the distant call of a wolf. Standing high on a rock in the light of a glorious moon stood a broken, defeated wolf. On wobbly legs, he began calling with a weak and muffled howl to anyone who would hear him. Serigala called to a scattered army of wolves, but none responded. The howl of the wolf made Captain Nibbles reach down and grip the handle of his dagger with his tiny paw. He knew that the wolf king would never give up, yet a smile came to his lips as he gave in to the deep call of sleep. He exhaled peacefully as he whispered, "It is finished."

Epilogue

Ichabod Percival Stump wobble-waddled toward the entrance to his pet shop. As he reached his key to unlock the shop door with his chubby little hands, he stopped when he saw that the door was slightly ajar. When he kicked the door open all the way, he found an empty and strangely quiet pet store. Every cage door was wide open, and every animal was gone. He called out sharply to Barnaby and only heard his own echo.

"Barnaby Bunch! What have you done?" the angry little man screamed. He walked into the shop to find a note left on the counter. He put his tiny reading glasses on his large round face and began to read the quickly scribbled note.

> Hello, Ichabod. My service to you and Stumpy's Pet Shop has officially come to an end. I don't think your father, Gustavo, would be very proud of you, but that is not for me to judge. I want you to know that I did not steal your animals. They all followed me freely.
>
> They will be living at the castle, experiencing the love, attention, and care that they all deserve.
>
> Most Sincerely,
> Barnaby Bunch

PS. Captain Nibbles wanted me to tell you that all the hamsters have unanimously and wholeheartedly forgiven you. Lola also wishes you the best and prays that you find help in dealing with your "baby squirrel" issues.

Ichabod was so infuriated that he crumpled the note into a tight ball and threw it across the room. When it landed, three crickets crawled out of a floor crack and sniffed the balled-up note with their spiracles, then retreated into the crack.

"Baby squirrel issues? I don't have baby squirrel issues!" grumbled Ichabod as he lit his cigar and began to toddle home. As he lumbered down the tree-lined street, a tiny newborn squirrel lost his balance and fell out of a tree and landed, unhurt, on the path in front of him. The tiny squirrel looked up at the old man and smiled. Ichabod began to shake and broke out in a cold sweat. He then turned and stumble-dashed for his life! Ichabod's screams could be heard for miles away.

The Lost Hamsters of Barnaby Bunch

Part 2

Chapter 18

Paffuto: The Five-Hundred-Pound Canary

Two canaries. Two eggs. Two nests side by side. Two mama canaries had been faithfully resting on their eggs for what seemed to be an eternity. They talked about everything under the sun for fourteen days while they waited for their babies to hatch into the world. To pass the time, every canary in their opera, or flock, was fair game to be assessed and scrutinized. Gossiping was always a great way to pass the long hours of waiting for the exciting first crack of an eggshell.

"It looks like Myrtle has put on a little weight, don't ya think?" asked Imogene.

"Oh, darlin', that train has left the station long ago," answered Edna. "She's tellin' everyone it's just baby egg weight; but, girl, she laid that egg three years ago. Those extra feathers ain't never comin' off."

"Any thoughts about *her* feathers? Natural or…dyed?" asked Edna.

"They look a wee bit unnatural to me," said Imogene. "But it's not *my* business. You know, *I'm* not one to judge, but those colors! Everyone knows, *red and green should never be seen*."

"Unless you're an Irish queen." Edna giggled.

"Well, that goes without sayin', deary." Imogene laughed.

The two mother canaries conversed in this manner for some time as they waited patiently for their chicks to emerge from their shells. Imogene's egg was hidden underneath her and out of sight as canary eggs are very tiny, weighing less than a penny or even a Ping-Pong ball. Edna, however, sat high above Imogene, resting on her massive fifty-pound egg. She was no longer keeping the egg warm; it was keeping *her* warm. None of the other canaries felt that it was proper to comment on Mama Edna's enormous egg to her face, but they all had grave concerns about what manner of bird would soon hatch. And you just know they were all talking about the massive egg behind Edna's back. That's just what gossiping canaries do. The next time you see an opera of canaries perched in a lovely tree, you can bet that they are prattling on and on about the juiciest canary rumors.

Early the next morning, just as the perfect flame of the sun ignited the horizon, Edna and Imogene were sitting on their eggs as usual when they heard the sweetest sounds of emerging life. Imogene heard it first, the slow, faint sound of *c…r…a…c…k…* beneath her. Then came a louder *crrraaaccckkk*. Imogene stood up and stepped aside to watch a tiny and beautiful red-frosted canary pop her head out from the tiny pale-blue eggshell.

"She is sooo tiny and beautiful," boasted Imogene about her own child. "I think I will call her Minuscola." Minuscola, or *tiny*, was the most beautiful canary that Imogene had ever seen. Of course, every mother thinks *their* child is the most beautiful creature that they have ever seen. Minuscola was able to manage a faint and dainty *chirp* as if to say, "I am so pleased to meet you, Mother." As Imogene continued to gaze upon her precious new baby chick with deep pride and affection, another sound erupted.

Crack! Pop! Craaack!

As the shell violently burst open, Mama Edna, who was sitting on top of *her* egg, was sent flying head over tail feathers into the air. She fluttered back down to the branch beside her nest to witness a gigantic, bulky bird head popping out of a shattered shell. A grotesque yellow head, which looked like a dirty giant tennis ball with a beak, turned from side to side, looking for its new mother. Its crossed eyes made him look dopey and lost. When the giant baby bird saw his mother staring back at him in shock, he let out an unpredictable, unimaginable, and ungodly *CHIIIRRRPPP!*

The whole tree shimmied and wobbled as the baby bird's chirp made the forest tremble. Mama Edna's feet gripped the branch for dear life. The force of his chirp was so strong that it caused Edna to spin around and around and around the branch as her tiny claws held fast. When the spinning stopped and Edna's eyes caught up with her body, she witnessed the giant swollen face of her new baby for the first time. He was absolutely hideous, but she still loved him deeply. No mother would ever describe their own child as fat and ugly, yet that is the only way her baby *could* be described. The canary chick's huge body was spilling over the edges of the nest, bending the branch that held him. The enormous baby canary was all fat, flab, and feathers. Imogene tried to console Mama Edna but couldn't seem to find the right words.

"He is…he looks…he seems…healthy?" said Imogene. Edna burst into tears. Imogene tried to encourage her a different way. "Well, he is very…sturdy." That didn't help. So she tried once more. "He is really not *that* ugly." This made Edna cry louder. "What will you call him?" asked Imogene, thinking that this might be a safe question to ask.

A very loud and rude canary from a neighboring tree yelled out, "How about Paffuto?" Chirped a bright-orange Italian canary named Rodolpho. The voice echoed through every tree and every branch, right into the ears of all the canaries. Rodolpho explained the meaning of the name in his Italian accent. "Ita…meansa…chubby!" he yelled from his perch. The other canaries wing-clapped and chirped their approval loudly. Everyone agreed on the name Paffuto, except Edna.

"Paffuto, Paffuto, Paffuto," they all chanted in unison, getting louder and louder.

This made Edna cry even more, but this time with an ear-piercing wail. She knew that the name Paffuto was an unkind name for her baby, even if it *was* true. No loving, compassionate mother would ever name her baby Chubby. But Paffuto wasn't just chubby. He was two hundred fifty pounds of pure flabby bird fat!

Edna wanted to name her newly hatched baby Caruso, Pavarotti, or maybe Bocelli; but the canary community had already decided on Paffuto. Minuscola, the other newly hatched, tiny, and delicate songbird, looked at Paffuto with both love and sadness. She felt connected to him, maybe because they shared the same hatchday, or maybe because her soul was filled with bright sunshine and eternal hope.

Chapter 19

Spectacle of Light

In early summer, the fledglings were beginning to test their wings. Paffuto had doubled in size and was now a whopping five hundred pounds! One marvelous spring morning, the sun's glory burst over the horizon. Golden fingers of light stretched upward, chasing away the dark sky. The forest was slowly waking up, and a brilliant display of life emerged. Hundreds of canaries were perched on the delicate branches of purple-flowering jacaranda trees. Tiny beaks were still buried in feathers, hiding their faces from the cold night air. The morning light revealed every color of canary imaginable. There were bright yellow, red, and orange canaries. There were green, bronzy blue, and cinnamon canaries. There were pink mosaic, red-frosted, and ivory yellow canaries. As the first light of the sun began to filter through the branches, a full rainbow of beautiful tiny songbirds appeared. Each canary seemed to glow and sparkle, and together they created a breathtaking array of glittering jewels. It was a dramatic spectacle of light and color. When the choir of birds began to chirp and sing, it sounded as if the gates of heaven had opened and the angels themselves were blessing the world with a new song of promise. If you were out for a peaceful walk in this forest at the break of dawn and came upon this glorious site, you would surely be overwhelmed by its splendor. Your very breath would escape you, and your eyes might even fill with soft, warm tears as you witnessed its beauty.

By contrast, there stood a lone pine tree, set apart from the beautiful purple flowering trees. It had brown and dying branches mixed with just a speck of green here and there. It was a patchy tree, missing branches altogether with big gaps to reveal dried needles and decayed old nests from years gone by. If your eyes followed up, up, and even more up, you would behold a very sad and gloomy sight. High up in the tree was the most pathetic-looking canary you have ever seen. On a heavy, thick branch sat Paffuto, a very round and weighty bird, perched all alone. He was a solitary bird with uneven patches of dull yellow feathers, all frayed and frazzled and sticking out in every direction. The bird's weight caused the branch that he was sitting on to bend like the spine of a weary old traveler. He resembled a disoriented balloon that had drifted aimlessly before getting tangled in the branches of the dying pine. How he grew to such an enormous size is anyone's guess. Five hundred pounds is *not* unusual for a young rhinoceros, but quite unheard of for a canary. The name Paffuto was not a name that allowed him to feel like a beautiful and delicate songbird. Whenever Paffuto's mother heard the other canaries call out his name with scoffing and ridicule, her heart was utterly crushed. She would weep for hours whenever her newly hatched baby was attacked with such stinging, hateful words. She cried because of the painful unkindness shown to him from the other songbirds. How could such beautiful canaries sound so glorious and uplifting when they sang and so savage when they attacked Paffuto with those same voices? When Paffuto was around, the cruel songs and taunting would always begin. This is what the other canaries would sing:

> Plumpy, lumpy, chubby, and round,
> Paffuto can't get off the ground.
> Tubby, blubby, pudgy, and slow,
> Paffuto's belly is made of dough!

> Chumpy, frumpy, bloated, and large,
> Paffuto moves like a river barge.
> Lazy, sleepy, drowsy, and dull,
> Paffuto's belly is always full.

THE LOST HAMSTERS OF BARNABY BUNCH

> Portly, pudgy, tubby, and slow,
> His head is filled with soggy dough.
> His chirp is a disgusting sound,
> Paffuto, Fattuto, chubby and round.

But not all the canaries were hateful and cruel to Paffuto. Minuscola, the petite red-frosted canary, was always kind to him. Her heart was filled with compassion, and her soul was flooded with kindness. She felt an immediate bond with the big canary that nobody loved. She never joined in the hurtful songs that the others would sing, and she would always encourage Paffuto to ignore their taunting. Cola, as the other canaries called her, felt Paffuto's pain whenever the others sang their hateful songs. When Paffuto's heart ached, her heart ached as well. Miss Cola was Paffuto's only true friend. She was the only one who truly understood him. She was the only one who believed in him, 100 percent.

Chapter 20

Angry Eyes

All the canaries were perched proudly on thin, bouncy tree branches to watch the world go by. They loved to show off their exquisite colors and rich, melodic singing voices. As you probably already know, boy canaries sing far more than girl canaries. I think it is their way of trying to get the attention of the girl canaries. Every chirp, chatter, and trill are like shouting, "Hey, look at me! Do you think I am handsome? I am really something, don't you think? Don't you just love my exquisite feathers?" It must be quite bothersome for girl canaries to hear the same things all day long. Sometimes they just want to sit on a comfortable branch and enjoy a beautiful sunset or maybe just visit their friends or chitchat with their mothers. Nevertheless, boy canaries just *chirp, chirp, chirp* from the moment the early morning sunlight begins to trickle through the tree branches. They show off by warbling endless melodies while the girl canaries trill the harmonies, if they are so inclined.

Paffuto loved to listen to the sweet and gentle canary songs in the morning. He often wished that he could be a part of such an angelic choir. After all, he himself *was* a canary. He *should* be able to sing with the other canaries. But on this morning, Paffuto forgot that he wasn't quite like the other songbirds. There he sat on a broad, heavy branch that was bending and straining under his massive weight. His eyes were closed as he became mesmerized by the beautiful serenade of songbirds that seemed to drift up through the treetops and beyond the clouds. Oh, how he longed to be a beautiful songbird! He instinctively tipped his head back, swallowed all the air that he could hold inside, then erupted with a most frightful and hideous CHIRP!

The force of Paffuto's horrific bellow instantly knocked all the other canaries off their branches, sending multicolored feathers flying about like splattered paint.

You can only imagine how angry the other canaries were when they collected themselves and stagger-fluttered back to their branches, but this time with only half of their feathers attached to their half-naked bodies! They looked as if they had been carried in the mouth of a slobbering cat, then carelessly spit out. Paffuto looked around and saw that all the canaries were now staring at him with very angry eyes. They were scowling with their little crinkled foreheads and glaring at him with piercing eyes and extreme outrage. Paffuto's face grew hot with embarrassment when he realized how loud and unmusical he sounded. He just knew what was coming next. The canaries sang out much louder and far meaner this time:

>   PLUMPY, LUMPY, CHUBBY, AND ROUND,
>   PAFFUTO CAN'T GET OFF THE GROUND!
>   TUBBY, BLUBBY, PUDGY, AND SLOW,
>   PAFFUTO'S BRAIN IS FILLED WITH DOUGH!

A brilliant sky-blue canary named Rubacuori was the first to speak.

"You are no canary, Paffuto. You *can't* fly, you *can't* sing, and you are hideous to set eyes upon." The heartbreaking words that flowed from Rubacuori's beak struck Paffuto's heart like a red-hot arrow. Paffuto knew that he *could* get off the ground when he wanted to, even if it *did* take great effort. When Paffuto attempted to fly, he was extremely awkward and clumsy. Everyone would stop and stare at the amusing exhibition, a five-hundred-pound bird attempting to become airborne. It took maximum concentration for Paffuto to take flight. He knew he couldn't sing; he knew he couldn't fly as well as the other canaries, and he was very aware that he wasn't a delicate and beautiful songbird. He even had trouble landing on a branch because he couldn't see past his round belly to his feet. In fact, he had never even seen his feet!

But it was the cruel, mocking way that the other canaries were singing that made Paffuto's heart ache so deeply. The only thing on his mind was to get away as far and fast as possible. Paffuto turned his head and let go of the thick branch that held him. He stumble-flapped away as fast as he was able, which was about as fast as a turtle moving through a mud pit. Away he went with hot tears splashing down his cheeks. Cola's heart was crushed as she watched her forever friend slowly flutter away. With much difficulty, he flew a great distance until he could no longer hear that hateful, horrible song, the song that made him feel sad, sick, and angry all at the same time. Paffuto flew aimlessly until he found a monstrous white oak tree with a strong and sturdy limb that could hold all his weight and sadness. Paffuto had flown the entire day, and now his shoulder wings were burning with pain. The red sun crawled slowly behind the horizon as the dark shadow of night began to crawl down his puffy, tear-stained face. When Paffuto had become utterly exhausted from weeping, he fell into a deep sleep on the thick, heavy branch. His snoring shook the tree branch, which vibrated the whole tree, and even the ground beneath the tree. Squirrels, rabbits, and even a young doe fled deeper into the forest as they mistook Paffuto's snores for an angry approaching thunderstorm.

Chapter 21

Alzati Sopra

In the middle of the night, Cola's frantic squawks shook Paffuto out of a very deep sleep. The enormous bird tottered and swayed on the massive branch as he tried to wake up and gather his wits. Cola trilled and chirped wildly while fluttering above his giant head. Because of her agitation, Paffuto caught only a few of her frantic words. He heard Cola chirp-scream the words *scratching* and *biting*, and then the one word that shook him out of his deep sleep—*bobcats*!

"Slow down, Cola!" Paffuto said as he tried to calm her. Cola continued to chirp hysterically. "Breathe, Cola, breathe," Paffuto insisted.

Cola took a deep breath before continuing. "Bobcats…in the jacaranda grove! They're angry…and hungry! The canaries need you, Paffuto! It's the end of the grove! It's the end of us!" cried Minuscola. Paffuto had no immediate reaction to Cola's pleas. He just sat there without reacting at all. He was still feeling deeply hurt by the canaries' hateful taunts. He seemed to have a cloud of self-pity and pride hanging over his head. The unforgiveness in his heart made him rigid and unyielding. He sat motionless on the massive branch because he couldn't focus on anything else except his own wounded heart.

"Did you hear me, Paffuto? They…are…going…to… die!" Cola screamed as her wings beat wildly in the face of the giant canary. When Paffuto heard Cola's anguished cry for help and looked deeply into her fear-filled eyes, he was shaken from his self-pity, and his unforgiveness began to melt away.

"Alzati sopra, alzati sopra," Paffuto kept repeating to himself quietly. "Rise above" is what his mother always said to *him* when *he* was at his lowest.

"Yes, Paffuto, that's it! *Alzati sopra! Rise above it*, my friend. Let's fly! They need you!" scream-chirped the little red-frosted canary.

Paffuto and Cola lifted their wings and began to fly toward the grove. Cola wasn't used to flying so slow, but she stayed with Paffuto and the lumbering flap of his wings. The cluster of jacaranda trees came into view under the light of a strawberry moon as they drew closer. As they approached the trees, they could hear a different song coming from the canaries. The melodious songs that the canaries usually sang to brighten the world were now squawks of terror. As Paffuto and Cola reached the grove, they could see six hungry bobcats circling the trees below the panicked birds.

The purple flowering trees were dotted with some nests filled with eggs, and some with tiny newly hatched canaries who were not yet ready to take flight. Mother canaries would never leave their babies. They were ready to face the hungry blood cats even though they didn't stand a chance against them.

Under the bright light of the moon, the hungry cats continued to circle the trees below, waiting patiently for the songbirds to die from fright and fall from the safety of the branches. The large paws of the pacing bobcats pressed heavily into the soft soil beneath the trees, leaving their prints, as their teeth dripped with anticipation. Cola recognized the largest cat as Sanguinaire, the legendary ghost of the forest. Sanguinaire was known to leave trails of damage, suffering, and sorrow while seldom being seen. He usually prowled alone under a moonless sky because he loved the darkness. But tonight, he was clearly training the next generation of canary hunters.

Sanguinaire was an old and grizzled bobcat with a very short temper. His lips were black, and his teeth were splintered and jagged from biting and gnawing on the bones of his victims. His skin was dotted with mangy sores, and his mood was marked by a deep, festering anger and persistent agitation, like an itching boil that never heals. Sanguinaire was a cunning and ruthless cat of the wild. If his sight was set on you, there was little chance of escape. He was an unfeeling hunter and a coldhearted killer. After a meal, he would use his claws to mark the nearest tree, deeply gouging the bark, like an artist proudly leaving his signature on a masterpiece. The thought of becoming his next meal hovered over creatures in the forest like a dark storm cloud. *Almost* everyone in the forest feared Sanguinaire.

Paffuto and Cola settled on a high branch with the other canaries, looking down at the circling bobcats. Bobcats are efficient hunters, waiting for their victims to freeze in fear, then drop to the ground or into their waiting mouths. They would rather play a heartless waiting game than exert unnecessary energy to go after them. But hunger was making them impatient. It wouldn't be long before the vicious predators would start scratching their way up the trunks and into the branches of the flowering trees. The canaries knew they had to make a horrible choice: either stay and face the bobcats or fly swiftly away, leaving their young to the appetites of the hungry cats.

"What are we going to do?" Cola asked Paffuto nervously. Paffuto looked at the other frightened canaries, all huddled together and expecting the worst. Then he looked down at the growling bobcats. Paffuto thought to himself, *So this is what it means to be between the devil and the deep blue sea.*

Just as Paffuto was trying to think of a plan, Sanguinaire yelled up to him, "My, what a plump and hefty bird you are. Mmm…so big, round, and meaty…"

"So you are the infamous Sanguinaire," answered Paffuto. "Such an unusual name, I must say. It sounds so…so rich and elegant. You must be very important."

"It *is* French, my yellow bloated friend," Sanguinaire said proudly. "It means…*bloodthirsty*. Yes, I am very important and feared by everyone. And you are…Paffuto? We have heard of you. You will make such a satisfying buffet for us," said Sanguinaire wryly.

Paffuto turned to Minuscola and whispered, "I think he wants to eat me."

"Well, that won't do at all," Cola replied. Sanguinaire was beginning to lose patience.

"Now, why don't you come down out of that tree, fat canary, and make it easier for an old, tired bobcat," snarled the big cat.

"Are you sure you want me to come down, Sanguinaire?" asked Paffuto.

"Of course, my flabby friend. You will be more than enough for all six of us," answered the bobcat. "With plenty to spare for leftovers."

"Well then…come down I shall!" shouted Paffuto. But Paffuto did not spread his wings to gently flutter down to the waiting bobcats. He tucked his feathers in, then dropped out of the tree like a five-hundred-pound boulder tumbling off a cliff. The bobcats and the canaries watched in amazement as Paffuto plummeted downward toward the ground. Before the cats could scatter for safety, Paffuto's body slammed the earth with a thunderous crash. The moment his heavy body struck the ground, the force of the collision caused the bobcats to catapult high into the air. When they came back down, they didn't land like delicate cats on four paws. They slammed awkwardly on the hard ground. There were three bent tails, two smashed noses, twisty bobcat bones, and six bruised egos. Six achy bobcats lay moaning and groaning and gasping for air. Paffuto was unharmed as his body fat cushioned him like a marshmallow being thrown against a river rock.

"You *did* want me to come down, didn't you?" Paffuto said to a dazed Sanguinaire. The large bobcat couldn't speak because of the pain shooting through his body. The stunned and stupefied cats managed to rise slowly, only to limp-stagger away from the canaries, back into the forest. They had to find a dark and quiet place to lick their wounds and contemplate what had just happened.

A chorus of cheers rose from the canaries. Unexpected victories cause the sweetest of celebrations. Even the tiny newly hatched birdlings were chirping their gratitude from their nests.

"You know they'll be back, don't you?" Cola said to Paffuto.

"I know," answered Paffuto soberly. He lifted his wings and fluttered slowly up to a branch that would hold him. But this time, he took his place in a jacaranda tree, with the other canaries. One of the canary leaders timidly approached Paffuto after being urged on by the other canaries.

"We are overflowing with gratitude, Paffuto. You saved us," said Roi Canarias, one of the canary elders, with tears in his eyes. "We have caused you pain and sadness with our mean-spirited songs and ugly tauntings. We are deeply, deeply ashamed. Please forgive us, Paffuto. You are one of us, and you always will be."

"I guess *we* can't move forward if *I* don't forgive. It might not change the past, but it does make our future bigger and brighter," answered Paffuto. He knew that the giant that dwelled inside of him needed to grow smaller and smaller and, hopefully, someday disappear. The load of unforgiveness that weighed him down was so heavy that only humility had the power to lift it from him. He knew that if only his wings were lighter, he would be able to fly much higher. And if he flew higher, he would be able see more of the world around him.

Chapter 22

In for a Penny, In for a Pound

After the excitement of their victory had begun to fade, Paffuto and Minuscola gathered the canaries to tell them the harshest of truths, that the relentless bobcats would never give up. Sanguinaire was the most persistent and ruthless bobcat of all, and as soon as the cats tended to their bruised bodies, they would return. Sanguinaire was thirsty for blood, and nothing would stop him. The canaries were no longer safe in the grove.

"They *will* be back," said Paffuto to all the canaries. "We must leave in the morning!"

"But what about the babies and our beautiful grove?" asked Roi Canarias. "What do we do? Where do we go? Are we to become feathered cat food?" The mumbling and grumbling among the canaries grew louder and louder as Paffuto and Cola realized that neither one of them had a real plan to share. They just knew that they had to get hundreds of canaries as far away from danger as possible.

Just then, a tremendous commotion erupted at the edge of the grove. None of the canaries believed that the bobcats could have returned this soon. Their hearts stopped, and they held their breath, with all eyes set on the rustling in the tall grass. The movement suddenly stopped. The songbirds were frozen with fear. Suddenly, out of the brush stumbled three clumsy otters, tripping, toppling, and tumbling over each other, until they crashed into one otter pile. Sometimes when otters play, they lose track of where they are and who they are disturbing. They are the kind of creatures that would start a game of tag at a funeral. One tangled body and three heads looked up at the waiting canaries.

"Hallow, luvs," said the eldest otter. "Excuse our rude and disruptive entrance. We do apologize for disturbing your...solemn gathering. We *do* get a bit carried away sometimes. We sadly witnessed Sanguinaire's attempted assault on your home, and we would like to offer our sincere sympathies *and* possibly our assistance."

The canaries gave a collective sigh of relief, although they couldn't imagine what assistance the otters could give them.

The talkative older otter continued, "Forgive me for not introducing ourselves. My name is Harrison Thaddeus Remington Otter III. But you may address me as Harry. Harry Otter at your service." The otters separated themselves, stood up, then brushed and licked the leaves and grass off their slick dark-brown bodies, just so they would appear to be a tad more...dignified. "And next to me, may I present my younger brother, Otter Melon, a strapping lad, wouldn't you say?" Harry said boastingly. "And finally, may I present on my left, our beautiful and wise sister, and Melon's litter twin, Water Kitty," he said proudly. "Kitty possesses the brains, Melon commands the brawn, and I humbly lie somewhere betwixt the two."

Harry was clearly gifted in verbal skills and cleverness. He could talk anyone in or out of anything. He boasted that he once sold a secondhand spyglass to a blind man. He was the eldest of the three otters and felt a keen responsibility to protect his younger siblings. As the three otters stood before them, the canaries could clearly see that Otter Melon, Harry's younger brother, was by far the heftier and taller than the other otters. You could see why he was the *brawn*, or the *muscle* of the group. Kitty was by far the most intelligent of the three. She was wise beyond her years and possessed a certain skill of using wisdom and common sense in the most delicate of situations. She tended to keep her brothers out of trouble with prudence and diplomacy. They didn't always appreciate their sister because they felt that she was somewhat of a wet blanket, choosing logic and reason over careless fun. Careless fun is what drives most otters, but Kitty was driven by a maternal sensibility. If the use of Kitty's wisdom or

Harry's clever, convincing words could not get them out of trouble, Otter Melon would step in and use his muscles to solve the problem.

"We are so thrilled to make your acquaintance, young canaries," said Water Kitty. "But I must confess, we were doin' a bit of earwigging last night. We couldn't help to overhear your brushup with the bobcats, those nasty, gnarly brutes."

"Good show, big canary," said Harry Otter to Paffuto. "What an epic achievement, I must say! Descending from the top of that tree to give those biters and scratchers a proper thrashing. Well, I've never seen the likes of it! It was legendary!"

"But you know…those nasty *biters* and *scratchers*, as Harry calls them, will find their way back here soon," cautioned Kitty. "Sanguinaire is quite a tenacious and unyielding chap. And I'm sure you don't fancy another appointment with those irritated beasts."

Melon wanted desperately to be as wise and clever as Harry or Kitty, but his words *always* came out wrong, like a young baker deciding *not* to use a recipe when trying to create a most delicate chocolate fondant. If you don't follow a recipe when trying to create a fancy French pastry, it's going to come out very wrong. No one likes a flat, tasteless pastry. And no one likes flat, tasteless words. But Melon never gave up trying.

"Yep, you showed 'em really good," added the awkward big Melon. "Kitty is right. Those blood cats will *never change*. You know that expression…a leopard…can't change his…pants," he said clumsily, while trying with difficulty to remember the expression. He was trying with all his might to sound intelligent.

"Can't change his pants?" Harry questioned while snickering. "Maybe that's because a leopard…*doesn't wear pants*!"

"Then maybe it's his *mind*," said Melon. "That's it! A leopard can't change his…*mind*."

"It's not his *pants* or his *mind*!" yelled Kitty. "A leopard can't change its *spots*! He can change whatever he wants, except *his spots*!" Water Kitty always grew impatient with her twin brother when he attempted to sound clever. And now all the *canaries* were growing impatient with the otters.

"We don't want to interrupt your family squabble, otters, but we do need to make a plan," said Paffuto. "We can't stay *here*, and we have no place to go."

"Yes, a plan is clearly your greatest need, puffy canary," answered Harry. "It's time to crack on! Let's all toss our brains in the same basket and see what germinates." Water Kitty looked at her brother Harry who was deep in thought, then at Paffuto who seemed to be even deeper in thought, but the answer seemed obvious to her.

"The castle!" she shouted. "We must get you all to the castle! It's the only place that you'll be safe." Harry hesitated because he knew how dangerous it would be to travel that far with such a large group of songbirds. Within seconds, the otters became distracted and were once again frolicking and rolling over one another, because there are some things even an otter can't change.

Cola whispered quietly to Paffuto, "Are you sure we want help from these…these…*guttersnipes*? They seem a little…undisciplined, don't you think?"

"They *do* get distracted rather easily, but what choice do we have?" answered Paffuto. "We need all the help we can get."

"But can we trust them?" asked Cola.

"When they are focused, they can be quite useful," replied Paffuto. "They are very clever, and they *do* know the forest better than anyone. Those *guttersnipes* may be our only choice."

Water Kitty overheard their whispers, stopped playing, and inched her way over to Paffuto and Cola. "We may look like *guttersnipes*, but our heart is pure gold. Harry has his own reason for wanting to help you. Oh, but I promise you this, if he's *in for a penny, he's in for a pound*. His word is his bond, and he'll give up life and limb to keep you all safe," said Kitty. "You'll see. We'll still be here come morning, and we'll be ready to help you."

Chapter 23

Beaks to the Grindstones

Harry Otter felt a deep obligation to watch over his younger siblings, Water Kitty and Otter Melon. When Kitty and Melon were newborn twin pups, the family den was viciously attacked by bobcats. The ravaging cats destroyed their home, and sadly, the elder otters did not survive the attack. The loving and protective parents placed themselves between the vicious bobcats and their three otter pups, as any good parent would. Harry Otter was able to guide his siblings to safety through underground tunnels all the way to the river, while their parents stayed and fought valiantly to protect them. Harry had been very protective of his siblings ever since that horrible day. A year later, Harry returned to the den for a day of remembrance, when he saw the deep slash marks on a tree close to their home. It was the mark of Sanguinaire. Harry was ready to help protect the canaries from another disastrous attack and possibly avenge his parents.

In the early misty morning, when Paffuto and Cola woke up, they found the three otters awake and waiting under the jacaranda tree, just as they had promised. They were not romping about or frolicking but waiting at attention to prove their worth.

"We are very much at your service," said Harry Otter sincerely. "We know a place where you can all be safe, but we must hurry." Cola and Paffuto looked at each other and knew they had no choice.

"What about the unhatched…and the nestlings?" asked Cola. "We'll have to find a way to carry them."

"Canaries are master weavers and nest builders, are they not?" asked Harry.

"They are," answered Paffuto.

"Then all hands on deck," said Harry. "Chippity chop! Beaks to the grindstones!" Harry Otter directed all available canaries to gather twigs, fine grass, moss, sheep wool, animal hair, and feathers. But instead of building more nests, they would be building *baskets*. The baskets would hold the unhatched eggs and the tender fledglings that were too young to fly on their own. The baskets would be carried on the backs of the otters while the elder canaries would follow in the sky. The songbirds collected sturdy twine from old nests to fasten through the baskets, then under the bellies of the otters to secure the carriers upon their backs. The canaries still feared that the otters were too absentminded and impulsive to carry their precious babies, but it seemed that they were out of options. Sanguinaire and the other hungry bobcats were not far behind.

The birds worked feverishly to weave two baskets. They weren't perfect, but they would have to do, considering their dire circumstances. When the baskets were completed, they were secured tightly to the backs of the otters.

Up in the trees, the eggs were delicately rolled out of the nests, balanced on branches, then dropped softly onto Paffuto's lumpy back as he hovered awkwardly just under the branches. When his back was filled with eggs, he gently fluttered to the ground where Harry Otter helped guide and roll them into the waiting baskets. Next came the nestlings. The mama canaries gently nudged their babies over the edge of their nests onto the lumpy and spongy back of the massive Paffuto. The tiny canaries were shaky and nervous yet excited for the ride down. The first tiny birdlings to hop onto Paffuto's back were the twin brothers, Dodger and Dawkins, then the triplets, Belle, Blimber, and Biddy. Bumble was the sixth, and Cholena was the seventh to climb aboard. When they were settled deep into his back feathers, Paffuto bumble-fluttered down to the ground, carrying the precious baby canaries. Once there, they were able to hop into the safety of the waiting basket. Cholena acknowledged Paffuto after she hopped into the basket.

"Thank you for saving my family, Paffuto," she said with tears in her eyes. Paffuto looked down at the helpless young bird now resting safely in the basket.

"My life for yours, little one," Paffuto said with a wink and a smile. Then he flapped and fluttered clumsily back up into the branches of the purple jacaranda tree to gather more and more fledglings. Tilly and her sister, Slowbird, were the last two fledglings to be delivered by Paffuto.

"Hurry, Slowbird," admonished Tilly. "Paffuto is waiting! He can't flutter by our branch forever. If you don't come now, we're leaving you here for a nice, tasty bobcat snack." Slowbird finally climbed onto Paffuto's back after she felt that her tail feathers were preened sufficiently and her beak was buffed and polished to her own satisfaction. "For the love of Alexander's parakeet, Slowbird," continued Tilly. "You're not getting ready for this year's Beautybird competition, are you?"

Many of the fledglings, like Slowbird, had no idea what the bobcats were capable of. They knew nothing of how clever and vicious the blood cats were, and they knew nothing of the dangers that lay ahead of them. Their lives were in grave danger, yet many of the young canaries were more interested in how their feathers sparkled in the sunlight and how beautiful their voices sounded in the morning. It would be up to the older and wiser canaries to keep them safe and teach them about all the seen and unseen enemies around them. Soon, all the fledglings were safely lowered from the peace and safety of their warm nests into a cold basket of uncertainty. Paffuto was exhausted after going up to the tree branches and down to the baskets so many times.

"I think my hollow belly is screamin' for a fair nibble," said Paffuto. "Fluttering up and down has made me quite dizzy with hunger."

"There will be plenty to feast upon where *we're* going." Harry laughed.

"Will there be pink plums and huckleberries, or maybe sweet grass and apples?" asked Paffuto.

"Of course." Harry Otter laughed. "As much as you can squeeze into your beaky gob!"

The thought of food made Paffuto's eyes open wide with excitement.

"Then as a famous wordsmith once said, 'Boldness be my friend! Arm me audacity, from beak to tail feathers!' What are we waiting for? Lead on, Noble Otter," said Paffuto with great anticipation. While Paffuto was dreaming about feasting on sweet grass and huckleberries, Sanguinaire and the other bobcats were dreaming about feasting on Paffuto.

Chapter 24

Morte and Morendo

Paffuto, the otters, and hundreds of canaries continued their journey of fear and uncertainty. Every now and then they would stop when they heard the spine-tingling sound of a howling wolf. The dreadful howl seemed to be getting closer and closer. Harry Otter led the way, occasionally standing up on his hind legs to sniff the cold air. He would lift his head high, sniffling and snuffling to detect any signs of an approaching enemy. Water Kitty trudged along on all fours, following directly behind Harry. The woven basket strapped to her back hardly moved and stayed secure with every step. The eggs were unmoving inside the basket, but the fledglings in Melon's basket squealed in delight with every bouncing step. Every time Harry stopped the procession, it gave the fledglings a few moments to catch their breath from giggle-chirping so hard. Otter Melon huffed and chugged directly behind his sister, often with his head in the clouds. Paying attention to his surroundings was not one of his strengths. Every time Harry halted to sniff the air, Kitty would stop immediately. Melon, in turn, would crash into Kitty's backside, which annoyed her tremendously. The fledglings in *his* basket chirped wildly, thinking that he was doing it on purpose just to amuse them.

"Again, Mr. Melon, again!" they shouted. Melon laughed with the happy tiny birds until he caught Kitty's cold, admonishing stare looking back at him. The adult canaries flew overhead as they followed the caravan below, while keeping a watchful eye on their babies. They were still extremely wary of letting irresponsible and untrustworthy otters carry their helpless babies. Paffuto and Minuscola flew in front of the other canaries as they scanned the ground below for anything that resembled a shifty fox, a lumbering bear, or a lurking bobcat. Wolves no longer seemed to pose a threat since they were scattered by Captain Nibbles and Barnaby Bunch during the hard-fought Great Castle War not so long ago.

They continued to follow a stream that most likely was born high in the mountains. The water was icy cold, crystal clear, and ready to quench everyone's thirst. Harry stopped and turned to the other otters.

"We'll stop here to give rest to our paws and wings," said Harry. He looked up at the circling canaries and called out to them. "Find an inviting branch to rest upon, lads."

The canaries saw the otters drinking from the cold mountain stream and understood that they were all stopping to refresh their bodies and their minds. They had been traveling since morning, and the skies were beginning to darken into deeper shades of purple and blue. The canaries clustered themselves in the branches of large sugar pine trees. Paffuto rested among the other canaries. After he had found the heaviest branch on which to rest, the other canaries began to flutter to his side and snuggled next to him on the same branch. This seemed like the perfect place to rest for the night. As tiny canaries nuzzled next to his massive body in the cool evening air, Paffuto finally felt like he truly belonged. As clouds began to gather in the darkening sky, the canaries nestled their beaks into their wing feathers, thinking that for at least for one night, they were safe. Cola, however, still felt uneasy. She had an unsettled feeling that nagged her soul. She felt that they were being watched. She did everything she could to stay awake and keep watch, but she soon fell asleep with the other canaries and the otters.

Cola's intuition was right; they *were* being watched. A very short distance from the sugar pines where the canaries were settling for the night was a decayed, hollowed-out oak tree that held two forest spies. Sitting on a dead branch, two repulsive turkey vultures, named Morte and Morendo, watched Paffuto and the other canaries drift off to sleep. The vultures were huge black-feathered birds with red faces and short curved beaks. Their cold black eyes seemed hollow. Morte and Morendo were scavengers, and they were hoping that a canary would fall from his perch during the night so they might enjoy a midnight snack. But they were not waiting in the dead oak tree to eat. They were sent by the wolf king to spy on Paffuto.

"Well, well, well," said Morte. "So that is the famous Paffuto." They watched Paffuto sleeping soundly in the sugar pine not far from them.

"Big, fat, and tasty," added Morendo.

"Well, just remember, we're not here to pick at his bones, brother. Serigala sent us to find him. He wants to know where the fat yellow bird is hiding, and now we know," answered Morte. "It's our job to bring him the news that he is waiting for."

"It's not fair, Morte. We're reporting to Serigala with drippy beaks and empty bellies," Morendo complained.

"Cheer up, Morendo. We'll try to find you something freshly dead in the forest," promised Morte. "Now, let's go give the good news to our king." They lifted their heavy black wings and flew off into the dark night.

Chapter 25

Bite of the Vipers

It was in the dead of night, when the moon glows brightest and the air grows cold and heavy, that Cola was awakened by a curious sound. It was an unfamiliar sound, like the stirring or whooshing of leaves, and it was coming from the forest floor below. The otters were on the ground, under the trees, sound asleep with baskets of fledglings and eggs still on their backs. They kept the baskets secured to their backs through the night in case they were abruptly attacked and had to make a sudden escape. All the canaries were still asleep, nestled together on the branches of the sugar pine trees, their beaks tucked deeply into their feathers. Cola noticed that the hissing sound seemed to be growing louder and more menacing. She quickly flew to Paffuto, landed on his huge head, and began to tap with her beak on the top of his thick yellow scalp. She tapped harder and faster until Paffuto's eyes blinked open.

"Paffuto! Wake up!" cried Cola.

"What is it? What is happening?" answered Paffuto.

"Listen. Do you hear that sound? That…hissing?" asked Cola. Just then, the otters began to wake up from the frightening sound that was all around them. The hissing was growing louder and louder. They looked up into the trees, and their sleepy stares met Paffuto's and Cola's widened eyes.

"Don't move an inch, Harry," Paffuto whispered down to the otters. "You are sitting on a *bed of vipers*!"

"What are vipers?" asked Melon in a loud whisper.

"Snakes!" Paffuto yelled back in a louder whisper. "Don't move!" The otters looked down to see hundreds of slithering snakes moving dangerously close to them.

"What should we do?" cried Water Kitty frantically. "I hate snakes!"

"Stay calm," cautioned Paffuto. The other canaries were beginning to wake up and began to panic when they realized that their babies were in danger. Paffuto released his grip on the heavy branch and began to flutter down toward the ground. It was difficult for him to hover over the waiting otters and baskets filled with frightened fledglings and unhatched eggs. The vipers were now hissing louder and drawing closer to the otters. As Paffuto now flapped and hovered over Kitty and her basket, he instructed her to release the basket from her back so he could use his claws to grab it tightly. Harry helped her loosen the basket from her back and gently laid it on the ground. They looked inside the basket and were relieved that none of the eggs had broken. With the edges of the basket firmly in Paffuto's claws, he began to flap his wings harder than ever. As his body began to lift, the basket tilted, and the eggs rolled to one side of the basket. They could only watch in fear as the clumsy five-hundred-pound canary struggled to lift a wobbly basket filled with dozens of unhatched canary eggs. Paffuto flapped harder and harder, his shoulder muscles burning beneath his wings. He flew the basket away from the viper nest and set it down carefully on a bed of soft moss, away from danger. Water Kitty bounded out of the ring of snakes like a delicate and gifted dancer, then rushed to be reunited with the egg basket. She breathed a deep sigh of relief after she inspected each egg carefully and saw that none of them were damaged.

Paffuto quickly flew back and saw that Harry had already chewed through the twine that held the basket of fledglings on Otter Melon's back. The fledglings were wide awake and chirping wildly. They were trembling with fear as they looked over the side of the basket and saw the vipers getting closer. Paffuto fluttered directly above the basket of fledglings, then opened his claws to grab its woven sides. The vipers were slithering closer from all directions. Their mouths were open, and their hollow pointed fangs were dripping with poison. While Paffuto was securing the basket in his claws, Harry and Melon snapped and yelped at the snakes to hold them back. They bared their sharp teeth to discourage the snakes from advancing. The canaries in the trees chirped hysterically at Paffuto.

"Save our babies, Paffuto!" they yelled. Paffuto strained and groaned as he flapped his wings harder than he had ever flapped before. This basket was more of a challenge to lift because the fledglings were hopping about, causing it to sway back and forth. He pulled the basket up, inch by agonizing inch. The fledglings in the basket were chirping wildly and clapping their tiny wings together, offering encouragement to Paffuto. While the big canary was straining to lift the basket off the ground, Harry and Melon persisted in snapping and snarling at the venomous vipers.

"Save us, Mr. Paffuto!" yelled one fledgling from inside the basket. As the basket was being lifted by the large canary, it swayed back and forth wildly. It began to twist out of control. It started to spin wildly, before slamming against the trunk of a tree.

Cholena, who was one of the smaller and lighter fledglings, was jarred loose and popped over the side and out of the basket. She fell headlong toward the vipers below. All the canaries watching from the trees gasped, looking on in horror as one of their own began to fall toward the waiting fangs of the snakes. As Paffuto held tightly to steady the basket, he could only do one thing. He chirped, "CHIRP!"

His alarming bellow caused the vipers to freeze in their tracks momentarily. Some slithered away in fear, but some remained, dazed and disoriented. But even Paffuto's tremendous chirp was not enough to stop Cholena from falling. The tiny bird continued to fall and soon would lie broken on the hard ground below. All the canaries began to scream out, "Fly, Cholena, fly!"

Then Cola joined in, "Fly, Cholena, fly!"

Then the otters joined in, "Use your flappers, tiny bird!"

Then Paffuto joined in the loudest, "Fly, Little Cholena, fly! Flap your mighty wings!"

So Cholena did just that. Her wings began to flutter, then flap faster and faster, then faster still. She had never flown before, but everyone seemed to believe that she could, so she tried. Her small beating wings immediately slowed her fall. Then she found herself suspended in midair! She remained six feet off the ground, and she was no longer falling! She saw the snakes below her, but she was out of their reach. She was fluttering awkwardly, but she was flying!

"Keep flapping, little bird!" yelled Paffuto. And then an amazing thing happened.

Cholena's tiny body began to rise. She flapped her way up to the basket, where her fledgling friends were chirping and cheering wildly as they witnessed Cholena flying just outside their basket. Then she rose higher to where Paffuto was still flapping *his* wings and holding on to the edges of the fledgling basket. She was now even with Paffuto and looking straight into his smiling eyes. She could see the pride on his face, and it gave her even more encouragement to keep her wings moving. Her flapping wings lifted her all the way up to the branch where the other canaries were celebrating like it was the Canary New Year! She settled on a thin branch, her tiny chest heaving, as she listened to the joyful sounds of revelry and jubilation! They were celebrating two victories. Cholena found her wings and had come of age, *and* she escaped the painful bite of the vipers.

The snakes were dejected that they had lost another young victim. They slithered back into their dark hiding places, mumbling to themselves and blaming each other for their failure. But they vowed that they would strike again. They would wait patiently for more unsuspecting travelers to wander by, then strike without mercy. For now, the vipers would wait patiently in their dark places.

Chapter 26

Cheese in the Trap

Sanguinaire stood high on a rocky overlook, enjoying the darkness before the sun rose. He tilted his head back, closed his eyes, and sniffed the cold morning air. His ears twitched back and forth, as he listened to the sounds of the forest. He bounded down from his rocky perch and joined the other five bobcats who were just waking up.

"The canaries are close," Sanguinaire declared. "Today, your bellies will be full."

***

It was early in the morning, but a lonely darkness still hung heavy over the forest. The otters were already awake, checking their baskets and counting eggs and baby birds. Their journey would begin early today. The fledglings were awake as well, cheeping and chirping and flapping their tiny wings. No one was able to sleep soundly after the late-night encounter with the vipers. Cholena, who found her wings during the viper attack, was excited to take her new place among the flyers and leave the basket. The other fledglings were not quite ready for the sky, but they kept flapping their tiny wings, hoping to fly out of Melon's basket soon. They would be soaring the skies next to Cholena very soon.

"Secure the baskets!" shouted Paffuto. Harry helped to fasten the baskets to the backs of Melon and Kitty. Cola continued to spy on the bobcats from the air. She came back, declaring that they were getting dangerously close. Paffuto fluttered down to the ground to share the bad news with the otters.

"The cats will catch up to us soon," said Paffuto. "They will never stop."

"We might not be able to stop them, but we might be able to slow them down," replied Harry. "Do you know of the Black Pond, Paffuto?"

"The Black Pond? What is the Black Pond?" asked Cola.

"It's not water, and it's not earth. It's a dark pond that sucks you in and pulls you down. It traps you in place and causes your heart to beat faster with fear," explained Harry. "I'm embarrassed to say, but we've had to drag Melon out of the Black Pond…twice. But that's a story for another time. Maybe we can use the Black Pond to slow Sanguinaire down somehow."

"I have an idea," said Paffuto, "but it will take great courage… and trust."

The otters were ready to move out. Kitty continued to carry the basket of eggs on *her* back because the canaries knew that she was more like a mother and would treat their babies with delicate care. Kitty's paws seemed to absorb the hard path as she cautiously moved forward, with the eggs barely moving within her basket. The mother canaries trusted her far more than the carefree and clumsy Melon. He was bumbling and awkward, but the fledglings in *his* basket didn't seem to mind. They loved the bouncy and jaunty way he traveled along the path. Since Melon had such a heavy and energetic bounce in his gait, it caused the tiny birdlings to launch into the air with every step that he took. They chirp-giggled the whole way and never tired of the bumpy journey.

It was hours later, trudging and tromping through thickets and clumps of brushwood, before Harry stopped. The sun was now high in the sky, but the forest below was bathed in shadows. The broad leaves of the chinaberry trees seemed to block out the warmest rays of the sun. Harry stood up on his hind legs and sniffed the air deeply.

There was a stagnant stench in the air, something moldy and dank. Harry carefully pushed back a clump of spike rushes to find a huge pond of black and sticky gunge. It was not a pond of water, but rather a foreboding mass of dark sludge. This was the Black Pond that only a few knew about. Paffuto saw that the otters had stopped and looked down from his perch in a monkeypod tree. Cola and the other canaries were perched as well, looking down at what looked like a pond of black water. Paffuto and Cola fluttered down to meet with Harry at the bank of the pond.

"The bobcats are faster than us, Paffuto," Harry said as he looked up at the massive round canary. "We can't outrun them."

"So if we can't outrun them, we'll just have to outwit them," Paffuto answered.

"So the plan is to trap the scratchers in this mudhole?" added Cola.

"Yes, that is the general plan. Hopefully Sanguinaire will have no objections," answered Paffuto. "But first, my tiny red-frosted friend, we must get everyone to the other side of this muck, then wait in plain sight."

"You mean you want us to wait on the other side of the pond and *let* the bobcats *see* us?" asked Harry.

"Yes. We *all* need to be seen, but especially *me*," said Paffuto. "I'll be the biggest lump of cheese in the mousetrap. We'll tell the other canaries that they can't wait up in the trees. They need to be on the ground to be their cheesiest. Those nasty scratchers need to *see* their breakfast and *smell* their breakfast. I want them drooling over a full plate of otters and canaries. Hopefully, their hungry bellies will be stronger than their brains."

Harry and Cola felt unsettled at the thought of looking directly into the face of death, but they reluctantly trusted Paffuto's plan. The bobcats would be staring at the canaries and the otters from across the Black Pond, with their stomachs growling and their sloppy mouths drooling.

Paffuto and Cola lifted their wings and flew back up into the branches where the other canaries were waiting for their marching orders. Kitty and Melon followed Harry's directions and began to circle the quicksand pond, cautiously walking along its bank. With baskets of fledglings and eggs on their backs, they were ever so careful not to slip into the sinking black mud themselves.

***

Sanguinaire stopped to sniff the air and listen to the sounds of the forest. There was a slight breeze blowing from the direction of the canaries. His pointed ears twitched back and forth, feeling every sound and smelling every smell. He stretched his left hind leg backward as far as he could, then he stretched out his right hind leg the same way. The bobcats around him growled slightly as they caught drifting scents of a meal that they would soon enjoy. The hunger in their bellies caused them to feel even more agitated and aggressive than usual. They were more determined than ever to finally overcome the fleeing otters and canaries.

***

There was no easy path to get to the other side of the Black Pond. So Harry, Kitty, and Melon had to be precise in their navigation around its banks. They would have to be very careful, rambling through the spike rushes and the cattails that grew on the edges of the pond. They were also heedful of the protruding roots from the black willow trees. One trip and stumble and they would fall into the sludge with the precious baby canaries. Slowly and carefully, they made their way around the dark bog while the elder canaries waited for them on the other side. The songbirds only had to fly *over* the pond and wait on the bank. Their bright colors shimmered in the late afternoon sun, as they waited patiently for the otters to safely bring their babies to join them. Soon the otters made their final turn around the edge of the pond and were greeted by a thunderous ovation of chirps and cheers. They were now all gathered in one place. There were Edna and Imogene, Rodolpho and Rubacuori, Cola and Cholena, and hundreds of other brightly colored canaries. And of course, in the middle of it all sat five hundred pounds of bravery named Paffuto, the biggest and most appetizing *cheese in the trap*. Everyone soon quieted down, at Harry's command. He knew that Sanguinaire was only minutes away.

"Canaries, take your positions!" shouted Harry. "Don't try to do anything heroic. Just be the cheese in the trap, ladies and gentlemen!"

The songbirds grew quiet and began to tremble as they nestled closely together on the ground at the edge of the Black Pond. They felt lost, not having the safety of the trees to protect them. The canaries stared across the murky pond, being tortured with anxiety. A smattering of frightened canary voices could be heard talking to themselves, but all saying the same thing.

"Be the cheese," whispered Roi Canarius.

"Be the cheese," whispered Cholena.

"Be the cheese," whispered Cola.

"I sure hope bobcats hate cheese," Melon whispered to himself quietly.

The terrified canaries were desperately trying to ignite a tiny spark of courage within themselves. Soon they would be looking straight into the haunting faces of the wildcats. They waited throughout the evening and into the night. Hours passed with no sign of the bobcats. They all took turns sleeping and watching. Watching and waiting. With each hour that passed, their nerves began to swell.

Chapter 27

Sticky Cats

There was still a layer of thick morning fog hovering over the Black Pond. It made it difficult to see the other side. The canaries remained quiet and watchful. Heads bobbed and eyes crossed as sleep began to overtake them. They were not accustomed to silent fear. They were born to sing with full hearts. They came into the world to make it a beautiful place for everyone, not dreading an attack by bobcats near a sludge pond. Finally, a single snap of a branch could be heard on the other side.

"Shhh…," Harry warned. As the fog slowly lifted, the canaries were now staring face-to-face with the bobcats on the other side. The cats had spotted the birds and were crouched in their predatory positions. First, they stalk, then they wait motionless, then finally, they pounce. Stalk, wait, and pounce. They were now low to the ground, ready to pounce and devour. As if it were a call to battle, Paffuto erupted with a deep and tremendous *chirp*!

At that moment, the bobcats, led by Sanguinaire, bounded straight toward the canaries who were waiting on the other side of the quicksand pond. The cats leaped toward the canaries with murder in their cold hearts. The canaries instinctively wanted to fly to safety, but Harry issued an order.

"Hold your positions!" he yelled. The canaries remained frozen, except for their wildly beating hearts. Their eyes were fixed on the bobcats who were now airborne over the pond of sludge, moving right toward them. The cats must have thought that the dark pond of mud was dry solid ground. The birds watched as the murderous cats slammed into the sludge, their giant paws sticking suddenly and firmly into the sticky grip of the slimy goo. The oozing mud held their paws firm, and they could no longer move. The cats looked perplexed and terrified as the dark sludge took hold of their huge paws, then their legs, sucking them deeper into the oozing trap. The canaries all began to chirp-cheer, and the fledglings flapped their tiny wings with vigor. Harry and Paffuto both gave a great sigh of relief and were very thankful that their plan had worked. The bobcats would be stuck for some time, and it would give them an excellent opportunity to escape. As Sanguinaire sat helpless in the sinking muck, his anger grew hotter as he realized that he had been outwitted by water weasels and songbirds. The other bobcats were angered as well, but they were particularly angry with Sanguinaire for leading them into this pit of embarrassment. They were once proud hunters roaming the forest; now they were just pathetic *sticky cats*. Five howling and screeching bobcats could be heard throughout the forest. Only Sanguinaire remained silent. He was already plotting how he would get even with Paffuto and the otters.

"A fine leader you turned out to be!" howled Nacho, one of the sinking bobcats.

"My belly will be filled today, will it?" chided another cat named Gato, as he continued to sink deeper in the sludge. Smokey, Scarf, and Stormy continued to struggle in the sinking mud, mumbling and snarling with displeasure at Sanguinaire.

"Shut your meat holes, you whiney scratchers! I *will* get you out of here, and when I do, I promise, you'll be eating otter stew with bird gravy! And for some dainty afters? You'll all have a sweet slice of Paffuto Pie!"

"And just *how* do you plan to get us out of this sinking mess?" asked Scarf.

"Don't you worry about it. We may not be able to control the winds, but we certainly *can* adjust our sails. For now, stop moving so much! The more you move, the deeper you sink," snarled Sanguinaire. The bobcats were dumbstruck as they sat motionless in the muck, their fur matted down, their minds swimming as to how they got into this filthy mess.

"So where are we gettin' a boat?" whispered Smokey to Nacho.

"There's no boat, you dolt!" answered Nacho.

"Then how are we supposed to adjust our sails if we got no boat?" asked Smokey.

"There's *no boat*, and it's up to Sanguinaire to *adjust our sails*. We are probably going to die in this mudhole, and it's all his fault!" said Nacho, glaring at Sanguinaire with contempt. The bobcats could only watch from the sinking pit as the otters and canaries began to move away from the pond *and* farther away from their hungry bellies. They were filled with disgust and outrage as they watched Paffuto and the others make their escape deeper into the forest and closer to the castle.

"We got no boat!" yelled Smokey to the other sinking bobcats.

Chapter 28

Wolf Moon

Paffuto and Harry were drained of strength after traveling all day, leading the canaries away from the mud-trapped bobcats. Kitty and Melon were bone tired, and all the canaries were wing weary. They decided that it was best for everyone to rest for the night. Cola flew one last scouting mission for the day to see if the bobcats were still caught in their slimy trap. She flew over the Black Pond and saw that the cats were still there, shivering in the cold sludge and snapping at dragonflies that flittered too close to their faces. She was excited to return to Paffuto with excellent news.

"We should be safe tonight. Those muddy cats aren't going anywhere," Cola said with a slight giggle. Paffuto was thankful that the canaries were safe for one more day.

"We can retire here for the night, but I daresay we shouldn't dawdle in the morning," warned Harry Otter. "Sanguinaire is a wily chap. He'll have all night to devise another dark plan." They all knew he was right. Harry helped lower the basket off Water Kitty's back and onto the ground. Kitty took great pride in knowing that not a single egg was lost or cracked along their journey. Then they both helped Otter Melon remove the basket from *his* back. The baby birds in *his* basket were wide awake and flapping their tiny wings, still aflutter about the exciting day they just had. Cholena had been flying for three days and now considered herself to be a certified master flyer, so she fluttered down to the fledglings to offer her expert advice concerning lift, wing angle, and flapping speed. Many of the canary parents also descended from the upper branches to see their babies. The fledglings would need to be fed before they closed their tiny eyes for the night. The eggs needed to feel the warmth of their mothers. So most of the canaries left the safety of the tree branches above and flew down to join the otters. Even Paffuto and Cola joined the groundlings below. Melon and Kitty managed to gather enough wood for a small campfire. Otters are very good at striking rocks together to make sparks. A small spark lit the tinder, and soon everyone had gathered around the growing flames to warm their fur and feathers.

"Tell us a story, Paffuto!" insisted an eager young nestling named Oliver. Paffuto would tell the baby birds stories at night during their journey to calm their nerves and lift their spirits before they went to sleep. He told them stories of great adventures, of brave hamsters battling brutish wild hogs, and the legend of the five stones. One of their favorite tales was how Wendell Cheeks, the hamster warrior, used his wits and courage to save two ducklings from an angry waterfall. He sacrificed his own life to save others, then miraculously came back to live again. The other canaries, young and old, began a slow chant.

"Stor-y, stor-y, stor-y, stor-y..."

"Very well, birds and birdlings…and noble otters. A story it is," answered Paffuto.

Cola sat perched upon Paffuto's massive shoulder, anticipating another epic tale. The remaining canaries fluttered down from the branches above and settled around the fire.

The otters had made themselves comfortable, lying on their backs under a starry black sky. Seven fledglings hopped out of their basket, then hopped up to settle on Melon's spacious furry belly.

"Once upon a time," began Paffuto, "the woods were ruled by a very evil wolf named Serigala. His heart was black as coal, and his soul was bitter as wild hemlock. His mind was dark and ugly, and he inflicted pain on anyone who crossed his path. Even bobcats trembled in the dead of night when they heard his savage howl."

All the canaries and even the otters were on the edge of their seats as Paffuto described the dark wolf Serigala. Clouds began to drift slowly across the darkening sky to reveal the ominous light of a full wolf moon rising. Everyone looked up as the brilliant light from the moon illuminated their campsite. Paffuto was just about to continue his story, when there was a sudden bone-chilling cry of a wolf baying at the full moon. The canaries shuddered, and the otters cowered together in fear. The birdlings that had been resting on Melon's broad belly slid off and bounced off the ground with tiny thumps. They all listened with rapidly beating hearts for what seemed to be an eternity. After a few minutes, the howling grew softer, then suddenly stopped.

"What…was…that?" asked Cuttle, a very frightened fledgling.

"My heart is achin' to jump right out of my chest," added Tilly.

"I'm sorry, Melon," said Dodger. "I fear I may have spent a penny while I was perched on your belly. That howl scared it right outa me." Melon looked down to see a slight trickle rolling down off his belly. He was much more concerned about the howling wolf.

"Everyone count five and twenty, then breathe," encouraged Paffuto.

"Was that howling just a part of your story, Paffuto?" asked Cuttle. "If it was meant to frighten us, it worked like a proper charm."

"I am afraid it *wasn't* part of the story. I am sorry to have to tell you all…but it seems that Serigala is still…very much alive. He is howling at the full wolf moon tonight to find his pack members and to gather them for hunting. But he is also calling anyone in the forest, to see who will join him," said Paffuto solemnly. "I fear that some of *you* might let go of everything you have ever known to follow him."

"Follow him to do what?" asked Harry.

"Anything his dark heart wants you to do," answered Paffuto.

"I would *never* follow that wolf!" cried Rubacuori, the sky-blue canary. "Never!"

"*Never* is a long and strong word, Rubacuori," counseled Paffuto. "Serigala's howls are quite charming, and his promises are sweet. Guard your heart, little bird. Guard it well. If you don't, you might find yourself following *his* path, and not your own."

Chapter 29

To Snort Another Day

The Black Pond still held Sanguinaire and the other bobcats prisoners. They were helpless in the slow-sinking mud. Hunger was making them weaker by the minute, and their bodies were numb from the cold, penetrating slime. The haunting screeches of the wildcats could be heard throughout the dense forest. However, Sanguinaire remained quiet and still as he sensed they were being watched from the banks of the dark pit.

"Quiet!" Sanguinaire ordered the cats. One by one they quieted themselves, and their ears turned and twitched to listen with the big cat. They could hear the snapping of twigs and the rustling of leaves. They all shifted their gaze in one direction, looking to the edge of the pond. There, on its bank, stood a monstrous wolf, staring at them with cold, dead eyes.

"Hello, friends," greeted the wolf. "This doesn't seem to be your finest hour, now, does it, bobcats? Master hunters, outwitted by water weasels and songbirds? Canaries are just tiny annoying gnats. And yet here you are, mighty cats of the forest, outsmarted and stuck fast in mud. I can only imagine how humiliated you *all* must be feeling. Such a very, very sad display, Sanguinaire. You have clearly lost a very embarrassing battle," mocked Serigala.

"Did you come just to insult us, Serigala?" asked the irritated bobcat. "We know there isn't one ounce of mercy in your bones, Big Wolf. We don't expect *you* to save us."

The wolf crept closer to the edge of the sticky dark pond and locked eyes with Sanguinaire. "That's where you are wrong, mud cat. I'll get you and your mangy friends out of that quicksand if you like, but it will cost you dearly," said the great wolf. "Are you and your sad group of paw lickers willing to follow me without question?"

"We will join your quest immediately, Big Wolf, *if* you rescue us from this slimy trap," replied Sanguinaire. "We have no choice," he added under his breath.

Serigala found a long vine that had grown down from a wisteria tree. It was long enough to reach Sanguinaire who was stuck fast and sinking slowly. Serigala used his powerful teeth and jaws to drag the vine to the edge of the pond. With a twist of his neck and a flick of his jaw, he heaved the ropy vine across the sticky pit, landing it right next to the bobcat's mouth. Sanguinaire locked his teeth on the vine, then Serigala pulled him from the hopeless pit of mud and dragged him toward the edge of the pond. With one more powerful twist of his neck and a swift flick of his mighty jaw, Serigala catapulted the bobcat out of the Black Pond and onto the bank. They each dropped their ends of the vine from their mouths. Sanguinaire never felt so small and pathetic as he looked up at the magnificent wolf. Out of sheer gratitude, the bobcat bowed down before the great wolf to show his allegiance. They continued to rescue the other five bobcats, using the vine to pull them, one by one, out of the mire. Soon, all the bobcats were standing on the bank, caked in mud but forever grateful to the giant wolf. Serigala was slowly building an army.

As the wolf moved forward with six mud-caked bobcats trudging slowly behind him, he suddenly stopped to listen to the sounds of the night. What he heard was the distinct sound of foul snorting and course laughter. The wolf king moved quietly, with six shivering and hungry bobcats creeping behind him. They came to a clearing where three fat wild boars sat around a blazing fire. The giant wolf and his new followers stood in the shadows on the edge of their camp. The wild boars sat around a blazing fire not knowing that they were being watched by the wolf king. The boars were having a colorful discussion filled with arrogant boasts and bold promises.

"If we ever cross paths with those forest rats again," declared Sir Walter Fat Belly, "we'll snap off their heads before we swallow their ratty carcasses."

"They like to call themselves…*hamsters*, Sir Walter," corrected Dingus.

"I don't give a royal road apple what they call themselves!" yelled Sir Walter. He put one of his hooves up to the side of his fat, gristly head, touching his ear. "'Aven't been able to hear a peep outa this sound hole since they shot me through with an arrow. Oh, they'll pay, they will…"

"Oh yes, they'll be payin' aplenty," repeated Butkus. "We almost had our gullets stuffed with sweet hammy treats before we was bushwhacked by those pocket rats."

"And now they be sittin' pretty in the wolf castle," continued Walter. "That weak loser Serigala just let those rodents dance right in there and make themselves at home. 'Magine that, teeny tiny hamsters throttling the king of all wolves, then kickin' his lazy carcass right out of the castle." The three wild boars leaned back and erupted with laughter, slobbering and gasping for air.

Serigala emerged slowly from the shadows and stood on the opposite side of the firepit, the flames flickering across his face. The eyes of the boars had been closed because they were laughing so hard. When they finally took a breath and opened their eyes, Serigala stood before them with his mouth opened slightly, showing his long sharp fangs.

The laughter and after giggles slowed to an awkward stop. The silence seemed like an eternity. The only sounds heard were the intermittent popping of hot coals in the fire. Finally, Sir Walter Fat Belly nervously spoke. "W…w…welcome to our humble camp, Your H…H…Highness. May we offer you a flagon of dark pearl tea or perhaps a ginger scone? Won't you sit and warm your paws by our fire?" There was silence followed by more restless prattle. "What brings you and your distinguished companions to our neck of the forest?" asked Sir Walter. "Have you…been here long?"

"We've been here for some time, fat pig," Serigala answered in a deep, booming voice. "My starving companions and I have been listening in the shadows."

"Oh well, looks like this is the end of us," offered Dingus. "Just a suggestion, Large Wolf, but you might want to start on Sir Walter first," he added, hoping that the wolf and the bobcats would be plumpy-full before they feasted on him.

"As much as I do enjoy a fine, sizzling pork chop by a warm fire," said Serigala, "I do have a different proposition for all of you, piglets. I understand that we have the same enemy. It seems that we were both outflanked by the same hamster warriors, led by a... Captain Nibbles?"

"That'd be the one," answered Sir Walter. "He was usin' some sort of supernatural charms. Magic stones is what reached our ear-holes. What might be your proposition, Your Highness, if I may be so bold as to inquire?"

"Join me and my kitty-cat companions here, and you *will* have your revenge. Follow me into the dark night, and you will live," snarled Serigala. "If you choose *not* to follow us, well, let's just say you are all invited to join us for a braised pork belly picnic."

"That's awful nice of them," said Butkus to Sir Walter. "We haven't been invited to a picnic for a long time. Come to think of it, can't remember if we've ever been—"

"You idiot! He's inviting *us* to be the *main course*. We're the pork belly!" answered Sir Walter.

Sir Walter, Dingus, and Butkus looked at each other and agreed immediately to follow Serigala. They were grateful that at least on this night, they would not be the main course at a pork belly picnic. The bobcats looked dejected, *again*. They were so looking forward to getting something, anything in their bellies. Sir Walter didn't care what evil he was being asked to join himself to, as long as he would live *to snort another day*. Serigala's new followers continued to grow. There would be one more night of the full wolf moon, and Serigala would call for still more to join him.

Chapter 30

Twister of Words

The next morning, dark shadows crawled away slowly on the forest floor, fleeing the approaching streaks of morning light. The otters woke to unusual chatter from the canaries above them. The canaries usually woke up chirping, singing, and preening; but today was different. Agitated and desperate squawking echoed throughout the branches. Something was very wrong. Paffuto continued to snore as his heavy body melted into the branch that held him. Gravity caused his neck to sink into his large round body. His head seemed to disappear into a bed of dingy yellow feathers. Each time he snored, leaves shook loose from the branches and floated to the ground. Cola fluttered down from a higher branch and landed right on top of Paffuto's large head. She frantically pecked Paffuto's scalp, hoping to awaken him from his deep sleep.

"Paffuto! Wake up! Canaries have gone missing!" Cola cried out hysterically.

"What do you mean…missing?" Paffuto asked while yawning.

"There were late-night whispers about the call of the wolf. They said the sound of his howl was haunting their dreams. And this morning, Rubacuori and Rodolpho are nowhere to be found! Other canaries are missing as well! I think they flew off to follow the wolf!"

"Serigala is calling anyone who will follow him," said Paffuto solemnly. "I tried to tell Rubacuori to be careful and to guard his heart. I'm afraid he wasn't careful enough."

THE LOST HAMSTERS OF BARNABY BUNCH

"And we have another problem, Paffuto," said the tiny Minuscola. "The bobcats are out of the Black Pond. At first, I thought they might have sunk to the bottom, but then I saw them following that despicable wolf."

"Comfort the families that have lost a loved one to the wolf's call and have the otters prepare to move out. We can't stay here," warned Paffuto. "We are in grave danger!"

***

Rubacuori, Rodolpho, and the other lost canaries stood motionless before the glaring eyes of Serigala. They could feel the hot air from the wolf's nostrils rumpling their feathers. The huge beast looked them over slowly while the bobcats salivated at the thought of tasting one of the tiny songbirds. They didn't dare attack the birds unless they had the permission of their new king.

"So *you* wish to serve *me*?" growled Serigala.

"We would...sir," said Rubacuori, the sky-blue canary who stood trembling before the mighty wolf. Rodolpho, the bright-orange Italian canary who gave Paffuto his name, was usually very talkative but now was silent before the giant wolf. The only sound that came from him was his spindly bird legs knocking together in fear. Sanguinaire, the increasingly impatient bobcat, continued to wait upon Serigala's decision. If the wolf had no use for the tiny birds, the bobcats would be ready to pounce on them. They hadn't enjoyed a full meal for over a week. Their hollow, aching bellies made them agitated and short-tempered.

Serigala was a *twister of words* and a master of manipulation. Rubacuori was no match for the wolf's cleverness and trickery.

"It seems to me," Serigala said slowly and thoughtfully, "that Paffuto wants *all* the attention from his tiny collection of songbirds. He can't sing, he can't fly well, and he is frightening to look at. So could it be that he is doing everything he can to get simple-minded canaries to follow him?"

"That's exactly what we thought," said Rubacuori. "Everyone is always praising him for one thing or another. It's always *Paffuto this and Paffuto that*. It is quite disgusting."

"And isn't it true, Rodolpho, that *you* suggested the name Paffuto? What a perfect name to mock that fat, ugly bird. You are so clever and witty," said the sly wolf.

"Thank you," answered Rodolpho. "But it was only a *scherzo*. What you call a *joke*."

"Ah yes, maybe a joke. But Paffuto must be very angry about that…joke, and he's probably been holding it against you all this time. Do you think it's possible that he might be holding a great measure of hatred toward you for giving him a name of such ridicule?" Serigala asked convincingly.

The truth was that Paffuto had completely forgiven all the canaries for their mockeries, but Serigala was a master of bringing up the past to cause renewed doubt and pain. Serigala continued his manipulation.

"So it seems that Paffuto has no use for either one of you, really," the wolf said. "In fact, he is probably glad to be rid of you. He most likely hates you both and couldn't wait to see you and all your little friends leave. Less for him to think about or care about, I suppose," Serigala continued. "Paffuto finds you worthless, but you would be very valuable to me." The seeds of doubt that he was planting in the canaries' minds were already taking deep root.

"Then it is good that we left Paffuto and those worthless water weasels," declared Rubacuori. "He doesn't care a fig about us at all!"

"You are so clever, beautiful blue canary. You figured out Paffuto's intentions all by yourself! Bravo! How brilliant you are! Well, it is obvious that good fortune has led you to me. Here you will find a safe and accepting home, with me. You will receive your rightful place of honor with us, and I will give you all the attention you so richly deserve," said Serigala deceptively. "You and your little feathered friends will now serve as my trusted eyes of the king. Does that suit you, little bird?"

"You mean we will be like spies in the skies? Oh yes, Your Kingship. It suits us *very* well. We are very honored to serve you. How should we address you, Great Wolf?" asked Rubacuori.

"Just call me...Master. That has a pleasant ring to it, don't you think, little bird?" asked Serigala with a snarl.

"Yes, Master, it rings like a church bell," answered Rubacuori. The other canaries heartily tweeted their approval. Sanguinaire and the other bobcats shook their heads not only in disappointment, but this time in anger. Once again, the bobcats would *not* enjoy the sweet taste of beaks and feathers. The blood cats' anger toward Serigala started to grow.

Serigala's followers continued to grow. He made empty promises to all who would follow him. He told the bobcats that they would work in the galley as royal food tasters once the castle was retaken. Serigala always secured the loyalty of his followers by appealing to their deepest appetites. He told the wild boars that they would eat out of troughs made of gold and would always be full of the finest slop in the land. He even promised a company of badgers that he would have the royal gardener plant rows of summer-crisp pear trees in the courtyard of the castle if they would follow him. Badgers, as you know, would give a right claw for a juicy crisp, so *they* followed without reservation. Serigala found it quite easy to hand out hollow promises. He was amused to find what little effort it took to draw them away from *their* path to get them to walk on his. Now it wouldn't be long before he would have enough followers to retake the castle and make it his own again.

***

After Cola finished comforting the canaries who lost loved ones to the call of the wolf, she lifted her wings and set off to spy on the enemy. She didn't have to fly far. Serigala was now leading a new army of angry beasts. Sir Walter Fat Belly, Dingus, Butkus, and an assortment of deceived followers were now only hundreds of yards away from Paffuto. They were quickly getting closer and closer. Cola flew to a branch that hung over the advancing enemy. She noticed that Serigala had acquired more followers since she spied on him last. Joining the fight was Jitters, a baboon with razor-sharp canine teeth who joined just because of the storm of anger that swirled inside him. He paced back and forth, anticipating a fight. There was a slippery and suspicious weasel named Jinx. Serigala loved that Jinx could tell lies and smile at the same time. And then there was Carcajou, a very lonely and isolated wolverine who seemed to be mad at the whole world and would snap and bite anyone who got in his way. There were many other broken creatures who joined Serigala's quest, creatures who were lost and searching for a way to find comfort with others who were just as angry, sad, and lonely as he was. This was no longer a ragtag group of disgruntled beasts; this was now an army. Cola listened closely from a hidden tree branch above as Serigala gave orders to his legion.

"When I give the signal, you will attack without mercy," Serigala said with an angry snarl. "You have all waited long enough. Fill your bellies until you are satisfied. They don't stand a chance against your cunning and skill. Do whatever you have to do, but no one makes it to the castle!"

When Cola heard his words, she spread her beautiful crimson wings and flew back to warn Paffuto.

Chapter 31

The Glastonbury Thorn

They had traveled until their bodies screamed for rest. Otters and birds all sweltered under the hot sun. The air was thick and heavy, and they were ready to stop and find shelter from the heat of the day. When they finally reached the top of a hill, a small open field emerged. There, standing humbly in front of them was the Glastonbury thorn, an ancient tree with crooked, thorny branches that seemed to sprawl in every direction. It was not a beautiful tree, but it possessed centuries of folklore and legend. There was nothing in its appearance that would make someone stop and take notice, but it did have a strange effect on travelers as they stopped to witness its meek and modest appearance. It has been told that a traveler who was on a long journey stopped for the night. He stuck his wooden staff in the ground, then went to sleep. When he awoke, the staff had sprouted into the thorn tree. The staff had been given to him by a very good man, who some believe was more than a man. The otters settled under its prickly barbed branches to rest for a while. An overwhelming feeling of peace and well-being washed over them as they rested under its branches. Even the fledglings on Melon's back were calm and silent as they looked up through the branches in quiet wonder. This natural sanctuary would offer them the rest and tranquility that they had all longed for, at least for the moment. But the tree offered much more than rest and tranquility.

The canaries delicately arranged themselves in the branches above, finding safe spaces between the sharp thorns. Even Paffuto found a sturdy branch to settle on, although he was too big to escape some of the sharp thorns. Red droplets formed on his yellow feathers where the thorns had pierced him, but he didn't mind, if everyone under his wings continued to be safe. None of the canaries sang out, as this place seemed sacred and somber. Everyone remained silent on this lonely hill, near the tree with the thorny branches.

They rested for some time until they all heard it at the same time, the approaching sound of the enemy. They heard growling, grunting, and snarling, and they knew that the enemy was closer than they had ever been. But it was too late to run. Serigala and the bobcats were already at the top of the hill, sniffing the ground and approaching the tree. The canaries and Paffuto sat in the branches of the thorn tree in open view. There were no leaves to cover them, only twisted, thorny branches. They were within plain sight of the enemy. The otters were exposed as well. They sat *under* the branches, resting on the ground, with the baskets of eggs and fledglings still strapped to their backs. Harry heard a quiet voice deep inside, telling him not to move. Paffuto had the same feeling, so he remained still as well. The enemy was now standing only feet away from the tree, but they were blind to the canaries and the otters. Serigala sat back on his haunches and sniffed the air. Harry thought it was very strange that Sanguinaire seemed to look him right in the eye but didn't make a move toward him.

"There is no sign of them, but I know they can't be far," said the big wolf.

"I have a feeling that they were right here," said Sanguinaire.

"Or is it your stomach, wishing it to be so?" replied Serigala.

Suddenly, Cholena sneezed a tremendous sneeze that she had been trying hard to hold back. It violently shook the branch that she was resting on. The other canaries that sat on the same branch held on tightly but had to flap their wings to keep their balance. Paffuto was stunned to see that there was no response at all from Serigala *or* Sanguinaire when Cholena sneezed. In fact, none of Serigala's army reacted in *any* way. Serigala could not *see* Paffuto or the otters, nor could he *hear* them. It seemed as if a veil or covering was placed over their enemies' eyes so that Paffuto and his friends would be safe. The Glastonbury thorn was hiding them! Paffuto decided to test it a bit further.

"Hey, Harry!" he yelled to Harry Otter below. "It's the thorn tree! It's hiding us!"

"I know, Paffuto! They can't see us! They can't hear us either!" answered Harry, using his loudest otter voice. Serigala continued to sniff the air, looking confused, trying to figure out which way Paffuto and the otters could have traveled. He couldn't figure out how the otters' footprints stopped at the thorny tree but didn't go any farther. There were no footprints leading away from the tree, and this made Serigala's head throb in confusion. He had no idea that the otters and canaries were only inches away from him. He looked up into the tree one more time, to see if the canaries could be hiding anywhere at all, but still saw nothing but gnarled, thorny branches.

Serigala gave up and began to move his legion past the otters to continue their hunt for Paffuto. The wolf king walked under the tree directly beneath a five-hundred-pound canary who was resting on a thick thorny branch. Sanguinaire shuffled behind Serigala and came within inches of brushing up against Harry, not knowing how close he was to an otter dinner. Harry's heart filled with a very dark rage knowing how physically close he was to the one who took his parents away from him. They all watched as Serigala led his army down the lonely hill, away from the Glastonbury thorn. Soon, the wolf and his evil troop were out of sight.

Serigala and Sanguinaire moved down the hill from the Glastonbury thorn, still on the hunt for Paffuto and his friends. They followed a cold trail; there were no footprints to follow and no scent of canaries to lead them. Paffuto and all the canaries chirped and cheered. They were thankful that the Glastonbury thorn protected them from their stalkers. Everyone was happy except Harry. Harry was enraged, still thinking about how much he hated the blood cat Sanguinaire. He was cut off from the celebration of joy and thanksgiving because of the hatred that festered within him toward the bobcats. Cola could see how distressed Harry was while everyone else celebrated their escape from annihilation.

"Paffuto, what can we do for Harry?" Cola asked. "His face is crooked with anger."

"There is nothing we can do, Cola. Deep inside him, the roots of hatred and vengeance have grown deeper. His hatred is much older and stronger than his happiness or joy," answered Paffuto. "There are no words to serve as medicine for his heart. There is nothing we can say that will relieve him of the anger and unforgiveness that he has been carrying. Canary songs aren't strong enough to break down the walls around him." Harry walked off by himself and sat at the edge of the hill. Dark anger continued to swell within him. The canaries' celebration of joy weakened as they noticed that Harry was not joining them in their victory. Kitty and Melon became concerned and fearful for their elder brother. They needed him so much and looked to him for stability and guidance. He was their protector since they were otter pups. They would be lost without him. They began to grieve for their brother and the pain he was feeling.

Then a different sound slowly began to drift into everyone's ears. In the distance, the sweetest notes of music could be heard, which seemed to lightly dance in the air. It went beyond their ears and straight into their hearts. The music caused the canaries to gently chirp in unison, and Kitty and Melon found their bodies moving in a playful rhythm. The fledglings flapped their underdeveloped wings, and even the unhatched eggs rocked back and forth in the basket.

"Where is that enchanting music coming from?" Cola asked no one in particular.

Kitty turned to look at Harry who was now standing and facing them. He was changing. The tightness and anger had vanished from his face. A dark cloud had lifted from Harry's soul. The three otters began to roll over each other like usual. They jumped, they jigged, they romped, and they frolicked. They were being as ottery as ever.

"That heavenly music," declared Paffuto, "is coming from the castle."

"It's an invitation," chirped Cola. "The castle is calling us."

"And it's the medicine that Harry needed," said Paffuto softly.

Chapter 32

Sky Watchers

The music from the castle made everyone's heart lighter, but they knew they needed to reach the castle before Serigala could catch up to them. As Paffuto and the otters prepared to leave the safety of the Glastonbury thorn, the sun darkened for a few moments as a drifting shadow passed over them. They all looked up, expecting to see a storm cloud above them, but it wasn't a cloud at all. It was an impressive flock of pigeons. Hundreds of pigeons! All sorts of pigeons. There were Portuguese tumblers, baldhead kites, American show racers, and blue bar homers. There were fantails, French Mondains, and a whole division of runt pigeons. There were pigeons of every size and breed, yet all were flying in a tight and perfect formation. The flock was being led by a very impressive sky commander. They circled the blue sky above the thorny tree before gliding to a smooth landing on the path in front of the otters. The lead pigeon, or flight commander, was wearing a brown leather Biggles aviator cap with snowboard fur earflaps, and his eyes were protected by RBW-issued aviator goggles. He was clearly the leader of this impressive pigeon squadron. He was a distinguished-looking Dutch highflier with many medals pinned to his flight jacket. He cleared his throat before opening his strong yet weathered beak.

"I say who is in charge here?" asked the stuffy flight commander with authority. All paws and wings immediately pointed to Paffuto. The commander moved his goggles to the top of his aviator cap, took a monocle from his flight jacket pocket, and popped it in his right eye. He looked Paffuto up and down slowly and cautiously.

"My, my, you are an absolute hulking ball of feathers, the largest canary I have ever laid my eyes on," said the commander. "What in the name of Aphrodite's dove has your mother been feeding you?"

"Hang about, highflier!" said Paffuto who was clearly confused. "You can see us? And hear us? We're not invisible to you?"

"Of course I can see you, fat yellow bird! How can anyone miss you?" asked the pigeon commander. "Are you daft, boy?"

"I don't understand. You can see us, but the wolf couldn't…," Paffuto said, trailing off.

"WHAT IS WRONG WITH YOU, PUFFY BIRD? Seems your head is full of stump water. State your name, boy," commanded the pigeon as he looked closer at Paffuto through his monocle.

"My name is Paffuto, sir," he said obediently.

"I see," said the pigeon suspiciously, staring up at the oversized canary.

"And I am Sir Desmond Hillary Fitzhugh, Royal Flight Commander of the RBW. That's the Royal Bird Wing. We are in service to Hope Castle."

"I'm happy to—" Paffuto tried to greet him but was interrupted.

"Paffuto is Italian, isn't it? Means chubby, doesn't it?" asked Sir Desmond. "You certainly fit your title, Rotundus. I see that you are rather thick around the middle. Ha! We flew in Italy during the Battle of Monte Cacciatore in '26, but that was many years ago. We *all* got a little *paffuto* ourselves during our stay there. I myself almost turned in my wings for the stuffed pecorino rigatoni but finally came to my senses. Italy wasn't good for our underbellies. There were more than a few good pilots who had to bow out of the RBW. Couldn't quite lift their bulgy paunches off the tarmac. Had to stay back in Italy, not that *they* minded much. But most of us survived. Those of us who got out defend the castle now. Day and night, night and day."

"So to be clear, you are here…to help us?" asked Paffuto, rather confused.

"Of course we are, round canary! I thought I made myself abundantly clear!" said the pigeon commander. "We are *the sky watchers.*

Guardians of the forest! Defenders of the castle! Protectors of land, sea, and air! Have no fear, the RBW is here!" On the commander's signal, the whole squadron of air force pigeons erupted into a perfectly synchronized recitation:

> You'll never have a single care,
> We're ever soaring through the air.
> If beasties ever trouble you,
> Call on the R B Double U!

When the pigeons finished, they gave a crisp and hearty salute, turned, and made themselves ready for takeoff. Sir Desmond Hillary Fitzhugh, Royal Flight Commander of the RBW, saluted Paffuto, the otters, and the thorn tree full of canaries before shouting, "We *are* the Royal Bird Wing, in service to the castle! We fly high! We fly true!"

"Where are you going, Commander Fitzhugh?" asked Cola in confusion.

"We thought you were staying to help us," added Paffuto.

"We've got a million sky miles to secure and maintain. We have no time to spuddle about! Our time is incalculable. We are the protectors of all!" shouted Sir Desmond. He then reached into his flight jacket pocket and pulled out a silver whistle in the shape of a soaring pigeon. It was attached to a long silver ribbon. He reached out and handed it to Paffuto.

"Wear this whistle around your neck, large canary. When you need it the most, blow! You look like you have ample lungs to make a go of it. This is a bona fide RBW whistle that only sanctioned RBW pigeons can hear," pledged Sir Desmond. "If you blow, we will show, through blazing sun or blinding snow."

And with that, Sir Desmond and the RBW lifted into a bright blue sky dotted with the puffiest white clouds.

Paffuto yelled after him as he took off, "Which way to the castle?"

"Go north, fat canary!" Sir Desmond yelled back. "Hurry now, Rotundus, those dastardly scoundrels have circled the hill and are right behind you again! You must have confused them temporarily somehow. Clever show! Keep them guessing, I always say."

Sir D. H. Fitzhugh and the Royal Bird Wing flew upward and onward. The impressive flock of air force pigeons would continue to fly straight and true, patrolling the forest until they were called upon. Harry looked at the whistle hanging around Paffuto's neck.

"I feel much safer now that we have…a whistle," Harry said sarcastically. "When Serigala sees our whistle, he'll probably run for his life or maybe even roll over and die."

"Well, I'll keep the whistle close to me anyway. You never know," answered Paffuto.

"I think that old bird just served you a fresh load of codswallop," said Harry.

"Maybe, but it's always a comfort to hope that someone is watching us from above," said Paffuto.

"I'd rather *know* that someone is watching us from above," answered Harry.

"Ahhh…a question for the ages. Which is better, *knowing* or *hoping*?" asked Paffuto.

"So what *is* the answer, Paffuto?" asked Harry in return.

"I guess it all depends, my otter friend," answered Paffuto, "if you want to *know* all things or *hope* all things. *Knowing all things* can lead to an abundance of sadness and sorrow. Me? I live my life *hoping all things*. Hope offers us so many more surprises."

Chapter 33

The Bite of the Trap

They had traveled north all day while continuing to look back over their shoulders. At one point, the otters stopped in their tracks. A horrific smell filled the air all around them. It was the unmistakable wafting stench of wild boar.

"That, my friends, is the putrid odor of a wild pig," Harry said with confidence as he sniffed the air. "The nose knows."

"Not just any wild pig," added Cola from a low-hanging branch. "That is the foul, moldy aroma of Sir Walter Fat Belly. If we can smell *him*, then the enemy is close."

"She's right. That horrible wolf and vicious bobcat are right next to him," added Kitty.

Harry, Kitty, and Melon were completely exhausted from the journey. The canaries were extremely weakened and worn out from trying to stay one step ahead of tragedy. But Paffuto knew they couldn't stop and rest for the night, as they could practically feel Serigala's hot breath on the back of their necks. A cruel and spiteful wolf king, snarling bobcats, and vengeful boars seemed to be nipping at their heels now. Paffuto hovered slowly overhead, desperately trying to guide the exhausted otters and canaries to safety. There was still light in the evening sky when Paffuto settled his weighty body on a large tree branch. From his perch, he looked up. What he saw immediately took his breath away. High upon a massive hill, under the setting sun, stood the Castle of Hope.

"Take heart, everyone! We're almost there!" Paffuto was happy to give everyone good news for a change. Everyone chirped and cheered when they saw the castle. But Cola, the sensible canary, immediately brought the cheering to a sudden stop with a warning.

"We have to keep moving! Those monsters are right behind us!" warned Cola.

Fear took hold of them once again, and they continued to quickly move on. Paffuto lifted his heavy body off the branch that held him, and the otters began to push harder and move faster to follow him.

The sun dropped quickly behind the thick trees, and the forest grew dark. The otters reached the bottom of the hill, stopping to gaze up at the magnificent castle. Paffuto and some of the other canaries were flying slightly ahead toward the castle when, without warning, the heavy sound of snapping metal rang out through the forest. The ugly, gruesome sound was followed by Melon yowling and screeching in pure agony. His back paw was caught hopelessly in a steel spring trap with heavy sharp teeth. Harry ran to him immediately and unfastened the basket from his back, then lowered it to the ground.

The fledglings looked stunned and began to cry when they saw Melon on the ground, reaching back at his trapped paw. Kitty looked back in fear as her twin otter lay broken and helpless, writhing in pain. Paffuto and the other canaries flew back to the base of the hill when they heard the commotion. When he saw what had happened to Melon, he shuddered inside. He knew that it was Serigala who had set the traps surrounding the base of the hill to keep others from reaching the castle. Paffuto's heart sank as he could see that the castle was so close, yet they couldn't move forward because of Melon's accident. They would never leave him behind. Harry and Kitty immediately attended to Melon and comforted him as best they could. They licked his wound at the point where the steel teeth had clamped onto his back paw, almost to the bone. He cried and moaned in deep pain. Everyone felt completely helpless. Kitty cried with him and for him, but there was little she could do. Harry tried to pry open the jaws of the trap with a sturdy hickory stick, but it wouldn't budge. He used all his strength until the stick snapped in two, and he fell backward. *The bite of the trap* was immovable. Paffuto watched from a large branch and listened to Melon's wailing. All the fledglings were now chirp-weeping for their huge otter friend. Paffuto took a deep breath and fluttered down to where Melon was lying in anguish. He bent his head down and placed his closed beak in a tiny space between two of the iron teeth.

"What is Paffuto doing?" asked Cholena.

"Just wait," answered Cola. Everyone held their breath and watched as Paffuto slowly opened his beak. His strong beak began to separate the jaws of the trap ever so slowly.

Paffuto continued opening his beak, and the teeth of the trap slowly came apart. The strained sound of creaking metal could be heard by the other canaries still up in the trees.

Paffuto's mighty beak opened wide, and the jaws of the trap opened with it. Harry and Kitty waited for the moment that the trap was opened enough to slide Melon's paw from its grip. As soon as his paw was free from the trap, Paffuto let it slam shut again. Melon was quivering in pain, but grateful to be free from the iron grip of its teeth. Harry wrapped Melon's paw with the leaves from a nearby mustard tree that acted as a sufficient bandage until they could get to the castle. Since Melon could only hobble on three paws, Harry knew that *he* would have to carry the basket of fledglings on *his* back.

A sudden burst of cheers went up for Paffuto from the canaries. But Paffuto quickly silenced them because he knew that the enemy was creeping closer and closer. They slowly quieted down, and soon the forest became still again, except for the sound of the approaching enemy. Branches snapped and leaves rustled underfoot. Paffuto and the otters could hear themselves being encircled by the approaching beasts. There were snarls to the left of them and growls to the right of them. Before long, they knew that they were completely surrounded. There was nowhere to escape. They looked up on the hill and could see warm flickering lights in the castle. They had gotten so close and yet were still so very far away.

"Yoo-hoo, fat yellow bird," Serigala said in a singsong voice. "Going somewhere?"

Chapter 34

No Whistle, No Chirp

Serigala was blocking their path to the castle. They would have to get by the wolf king in order to reach their desired haven. The heartless Sanguinaire and the other bobcats were blocking them on the south. Escaping through a wall of brutal, starving bobcats was impossible. They were poised to pounce and devour. To the east of them sat the three wild boars, Sir Walter Fat Belly, Dingus, and Butkus. They stood guard with sharpened hooves and razor-sharp tusks. They were still angry that a band of hamsters outwitted them not very long ago. It would not happen again. They would not be outfoxed by an overgrown canary and three distracted otters. And the west was guarded by the other dark followers that Serigala had picked up along the way. There were Jitters, the baboon with sharp canine teeth; Jinx, the shifty weasel; and Carcajou, the cantankerous and carnivorous wolverine.

"We'll cover the western flank. No one will get by us," vowed Carcajou. "Let them try. They'll wish they were never born."

"Remember, bobcats get the fat yellow bird," declared Sanguinaire. "We have waited long enough!" He said this while licking his black lips.

"I don't care who eats who," boomed Serigala. "Just don't let any of them escape to the castle. The castle grows stronger every time someone crosses the drawbridge. Destroy every last one of them!" As the beasts began to move in closer from all sides, making the circle smaller and tighter, the otters and the canaries huddled closer together, trembling in fear and fearing the worst.

"It has been an honor knowing you from nest to grave, Paffuto," said Minuscola.

"You have been the delight of my heart, Cola. But this is not the end! Hope is believing in the smallest flicker of light when everyone else is sinking in darkness. Hope is full of surprises!" shouted Paffuto.

"I sure hope that flicker of light believes in you, 'cause I'm only seeing the darkest shade of dark," chirped Cola.

"As long as I have a voice, I have hope. Stand back and hold on to your little red feathers, my friend," said Paffuto. And with that, Paffuto took the deepest breath and let out an earth-shattering CHIRP!

But Sanguinaire was clever and had warned his followers about Paffuto's extraordinary ability to thunder chirp. They were well prepared by filling their ears with melted honeycomb wax so the sound of his chirp would be muffled and hushed inside their heads. Paffuto was baffled that the enemy continued to advance toward them. He felt the ribboned whistle still dangling around his thick neck and remembered Sir Desmond's words: "If you blow, we will show, through blazing sun or blinding snow." So blow he did, with all his might.

Cola's hope turned to dejection as she watched Paffuto blowing the whistle with all his might, yet the whistle made no sound. *We are truly doomed*, she thought. Paffuto's chirp seemed powerless. Sir Desmond's whistle was silent.

> No whistle, no chirp, no help from above,
> No mercy, no grace, no measure of love.
> How long do we linger, how long do we wait?
> Surrounded by enemies, encompassed by hate.

But Paffuto's magnificent chirp *was* heard indeed, not by the enemies who surrounded them, but inside the ancient walls of the castle. In the highest tower of the castle, a very courageous and vigilant hamster named Captain Nibbles was waiting for this moment. The echo of Paffuto's chirp filled his ears, as well as throughout every room in the castle. Barnaby Bunch heard it up in the Keep. Even Ratafia and the other castle rats heard the chirp inside the crevices of its musty walls. It could even be heard all the way down in the oubliette, the deepest, darkest dungeon in the castle, even though the Ouboo would never be used for prisoners again. Anyone who came to the castle now came of their own free will.

Captain Nibbles knew that help was needed as soon as he heard Paffuto's chirp. He ordered the monkey trumpeters to sound the alarm. Three golden tamarins stood on the ancient wall and blasted their trumpets in unison. The unified sound of the trumpets echoed through the forest; and every creature, both evil *and* good, stopped to listen.

Sir Desmond and the Royal Bird Wing had never heard a chirp, a whistle, and castle trumpets in such rapid succession. The sounds together were a call for help and a call to battle. When all three sounds reached the ears of the RBW, they stopped in midair and waited for their orders.

"Advance to the fray!" shouted Sir Desmond Hillary Fitzhugh. "Engage HWV!" The pigeon pilots all knew that HWV stood for *hummingbird wing velocity* and was only used in the most desperate of circumstances. The RBW immediately turned wing, then maximized their flapping speed to come to the aid of Paffuto and his friends. Sir Desmond sounded the order over the loud humming of accelerated wing flapping:

"Remember the signals, Birdmen! Your command is 'Guns, guns, guns' for the first volley! When you hear 'Double guns, double guns,' commence with the second volley!" Sir Desmond yelled over the deafening buzz of their beating wings. Then he looked into the eyes of his chief bombardier who was standing by, waiting for his orders.

"And for the final blow, the code word is *pickle*! Prepare to evacuate! Fly straight and fly true! We are the R...B...Double U!" Sir Desmond shouted as they all turned and flew to the fight.

Chapter 35

Archers, Loose!

In the castle, Captain Nibbles had already given the command for the archers to assemble. Seven hamster archers were ready and armed with silver-tipped needle arrows. Chewy, Two-Spots, Corky, and Tobias Von Schnee (from the Bavarian hamster clan, who was also a member of the Royal Bavarian Archery Brigade) were standing at the ready. The sister warriors, Lola and Rosie, were prepared and waiting as well. They were all being led by Wendell Cheeks, Hamster Warrior. The drawbridge was slowly lowered, and the hamster archers scampered across the ancient wooden bridge. They were swift of foot to make their way through the dense forest. After they left the castle, a mighty silverback gorilla named Archimedes operated the windlass in the gatehouse, causing the thick chains to raise the moat bridge and secure the castle gate. The golden gyrfalcon flew from his perch in the high tower to sail into the night sky. He would locate the battle for the advancing hamster archers. Once he found the location where Paffuto and the other canaries were surrounded, he would circle the sky in small tight circles, and the hamsters could locate them in the night forest below.

***

As Serigala and his army surrounded Paffuto and the canaries, he could have ordered an attack in the blink of an eye, but he had the cruel habit of toying with his victims before the final blow. This annoyed Sanguinaire, the starving bobcat exceedingly, as he was not accustomed to waging this kind of assault on his prey. He enjoyed the pounce and devour method of attack. Serigala was led by his twisted mind and cold heart, while Sanguinaire was led by his stomach and thirst for blood.

"Just end them, Serigala! We've waited long enough!" growled Sanguinaire.

"Do you dare give an order to the wolf king?" answered Serigala. "Know your place, swamp cat!" scolded Serigala, reminding Sanguinaire that it was he who saved the bobcats from the Black Pond. Serigala stared right into the glowing eyes of Sanguinaire. Suddenly, Serigala's focus was not on the fat canary or the otters, but on the large bobcat who seemed to be challenging him.

"Who are *you* to decide when *we* eat?" snapped Sanguinaire. The other bobcats formed a line next to *their* leader, joining *him* in challenging the wolf king.

"Maybe," answered Serigala, "I will feast on six bobcats tonight instead of otters and tiny birds. You might be far more satisfying." Just as Serigala and the six bobcats were facing off in a position of attack, Sir Walter Fat Belly took matters into his own hands, charging at Paffuto and the canaries from the east of the circle. Carcajou, the wolverine, didn't want to be left out of the slaughter; so he charged from the west with Jitters and Jinx. They all thought that they would surely starve if they continued to wait for Serigala's orders. None of them trusted or respected the wolf any longer. Paffuto spread his wings wide; and all the canaries, young and old, gathered under them for protection. The otters stood between the enemy and the baskets of eggs and fledglings and bared their teeth to protect them. Just as destruction was upon them, a shout could be heard from just beyond the tree line.

"Archers, notch!" shouted Wendell Cheeks. "Archers, draw! Archers, loose!"

Immediately seven needle arrows whizzed through the night air toward the enemy. The first one struck Sir Walter Fat Belly inside his good ear.

"Son of a blackberry!" Sir Walter squealed in pain. "Not again!" The next arrow struck Sanguinaire right on the tip of his black nose. His high-pitched screech could be heard throughout the forest. Seven arrows hit their mark. Rosie and her sister, Lola, both aimed at Carcajou, the wolverine. Both of their arrows hit the mark, one in the right ear and one in his left hindquarters.

"Coup de Croupe!" shouted Lola, as she held her bow high over her head in victory.

"Yes! High marks for a perfect rump shot, sister!" yelled Rosie.

Carcajou gnashed at the night air in sheer agony. He quickly decided the pain wasn't worth the fight. He staggered away and disappeared into the dense forest. The hamsters reloaded their bows with silver-tipped arrows and fired a second round. Three hit Serigala, but they were not much more than an annoyance to him. He turned and pulled the arrows out of his flank, using his teeth. Paffuto tightened his grip on the canaries hiding under his wings. He held them ever close, promising not to let them go. A third and a fourth volley of arrows found their marks. Chewy, Two-Spots, Corky, and Toby were dead-on with their aim. Chewy noticed that the arrows didn't seem to be affecting Serigala. So he pulled out a small flask from his inner vest pocket. It held the poisonous juice of creeper berries. He dipped the tip of his arrow in the mouth of the flask until it touched the poisonous juice. The arrows would not kill the wolf but would cause severe pain and irritation. Two-Spots ate a creeper berry once, and it set his mouth and insides on fire. He jumped headfirst into a butterfish pond with his mouth wide open just to quench the fire on his tongue.

After dipping the arrow tip in the berry poison, Chewy took careful aim at Serigala's back leg. He pulled back the bowstring, then released it. The arrow sailed through the night air before sticking fast in the wolf's leg. He began to howl uncontrollably as the poison and heat spread up his leg, all the way to his hip. He staggered about, dragging his numb leg, as he moved closer to Paffuto and the canaries. Serigala's eyes were fiery red, blazing with anger. He was now only feet away from Paffuto. He continued to stagger slowly toward the big canary, dragging his leg. With his lips curled, he bared his deadly teeth. The canaries and the otters gathered closer together under Paffuto's wings. But the canaries and the otters didn't tremble or fear. With the wolf inching closer and closer, the canaries began to sing! They chirped and sang the most beautiful melody of thankfulness. Even the otters rejoiced with the canaries. Melon sang like an ailing seal, but he sang! No one even laughed at him, except his sister, Kitty, who snickered just a bit. Even though there was horror all around them, they were at peace under the shadow of Paffuto's wings.

Paffuto instinctively prepared to erupt with the most forceful and deafening chirp his body had ever created. He took the deepest breath and held it until Serigala was only inches from his beak, then...

Chirrrrp!

The force of Paffuto's chirp blew most of Serigala's fur right off his body! He looked like a sheep that had just been shorn. His majestic dark coat was now blowing through the forest in hundreds of directions, causing a blinding blizzard of black fur. He stood there, visibly shaken and naked as a mole rat. He shivered uncontrollably as the cold night wind stung his naked body.

The hamster archers paused their assault momentarily when the steady sound of a droning buzz filled their ears. They soon realized that the sound was being caused by the steady flapping of wings. In the distance, they could see Sir Desmond Hillary Fitzhugh and hundreds of pigeon pilots flying under the light of a full moon. This encouraged the hamster archers to continue their assault, knowing that they would now be receiving support from the sky. Moments later, the squadron of pigeons was directly over their targets. Sir Desmond prepared the order for the first volley.

"Prepare to drop the jubilees!" Commander Fitzhugh ordered his flyers. Each of the RBW pilots was loaded with two very ripe jubilee tomatoes. They gripped the tomatoes gingerly in their talons so they wouldn't explode until they hit their mark.

"Locate your target!" yelled Sir Desmond as he flew them in position. "Steady...steadddy...aim...guns, guns, guns!"

Hundreds of jubilee tomatoes rained from the night sky. Everything was quiet except for the sound of hundreds of tomatoes whizzing down from above. This caused Serigala to momentarily stop the attack. It was a sound that the attacking beasts had never heard before. Then the jubilees began to strike. The hits were precise and effective. The tomatoes were dropped from such a terrific height that they caused immediate pain when juice and seeds exploded as they hit their targets. Paffuto could hear yelping and moaning everywhere as the tomatoes continued to drop from the sky. The pigeons struck with precision. Not a single jubilee hit Paffuto, the otters, or any of the canaries. Sir Walter Fat Belly and the other boars started to bolt for the cover of the forest with growing welts all over their bodies, but Serigala howled loudly and ordered them back to the fight. The wolf and his army shook off the first volley even though they were battered and bruised. They regrouped and set their eyes once again on their prey. Up above, the pigeons circled the sky and found their targets once again.

"Begin Operation Whitewash! Steady...steadddy...aim!" shouted Sir Desmond. The pigeon highfliers took their aim. "Double guns, double guns!" shouted their commander. At that moment, the RBW evacuated themselves with enthusiasm and precision. Thick white and watery pigeon droppings fell from the sky with pinpoint accuracy. The first to receive the RBW whitewashing was Dingus, the wild boar. It covered his head and his back and dripped down all four of his legs. A perfect strike! Next was his comrade Butkus. A direct hit splattered his snout and dripped down his forehead and into his eyes! He was blinded and ran headlong into an ironwood tree. Staggering to his feet, he was hit again and again and again from the air and covered from tusk to toenail with avian excreta. It slowed him down as it began to dry in the night air. It was thick and heavy on his body, which made him sluggish and tired. *I will rest for only a moment*, he thought. But as soon as he stopped, he froze in that position, like a gargoyle guarding the Bamburgh Castle. The squadron continued their assault, covering bobcats, wild boars, baboons, and weasels. No one was spared! Sir Walter Fat Belly was particularly hit hard, and it took many pigeons to pass over him before he became an alabaster garden statue. Some of the enemy escaped into the forest, never to be heard from again. They fled for their lives, but their allegiance to Serigala had already weakened, and they would always follow someone new, depending on which way the wind blew.

Sir Desmond and his squadron of deadly sharpshooters continued to circle above the battlefield. Serigala had gathered himself and was still intent on destroying Paffuto and the otters. The wolf king was angrier than ever. He looked different without his royal coat of black fur. He was naked down to his pinkish skin and wearing only a snarl now. But his teeth were still razor sharp, and his heart was darker than ever.

"I am the true king and the rightful heir to the throne and the castle, fat bird!" he screamed at Paffuto. Serigala lied so often that he now believed his own lies.

"You stole it, naked wolf," answered Paffuto. "And you are trying to steal it again!"

As Sir Desmond located his target from the air, one word echoed throughout the night forest. Sir Desmond turned back to his squadron and shouted an unmistakable command.

"Pickle!" he commanded.

Knowing that "Pickle" was the command for the final blow, a large swollen pigeon was brought up from the rear of the squadron to administer the final drop. He had been holding back for this very moment. His job was to eat berries and seeds for weeks, building up a formidable payload until he could barely get off the runway. He was the CB, the chief bombardier, and his job was to deliver the fatal blow. Called to the head of the V formation, the CB flew to the front to join Sir Desmond.

"You know what to do, CB," said Sir Desmond.

"I do, sir, but it won't be pretty," answered CB.

"It never is, CB. It never is," said Sir Desmond as he flew to the side to give him space to operate. At that moment, CB released a payload of fury that dropped out of the sky like a river of wet concrete. Down, down, down it poured until it hit Serigala with the force of a thousand seabirds. He was covered in an instant from his black nose to his pink tail. He didn't even have a chance to move from the spot where he was threatening Paffuto. Not a single white drop landed on Paffuto's yellow feathers. CB's aim was straight and true. To this day, if you are ever struck by a pigeon's wrath, know that it is with pinpoint accuracy that you have been targeted. The RBW is trained well. They are skillful. They are precise.

When the pungent white dust had settled, Harry, Kitty, and Melon joined Paffuto to make sure all the canaries were safe and accounted for. The hamster archers stepped out from the shadow of the trees, looked to the sky, and saluted Sir Desmond and the squadron of bombardiers as they flew off as silhouettes against a bright white moon.

After Wendell Cheeks and his band of archer warriors greeted Paffuto, they all walked across the battlefield cautiously and somberly. It was a great victory, yet they showed respect for a defeated enemy. Serigala, Sanguinaire, Sir Walter Fat Belly, and many others stood motionless, like baked white statues. They were frozen in time; their last expression was sealed on their ghastly faces forever.

Wendell and the other hamsters led Paffuto and his friends away from the battlefield and the chilling colorless statues that remained there. There was still one more hill to climb, but it would have to wait until morning. The battle made everyone exhausted, and it was dangerous to try to navigate the hill in the darkness.

"Is tomorrow our Castle Day? Is it, Mr. Paffuto?" Cuttle, the fledgling, asked excitedly.

"Yes, Cuttle. Tomorrow is our Castle Day," promised Paffuto.

Chapter 36

Pardon et Repos

In the very early morning, just as the blackish sky gave way to swirly pinks and blues, Cola flew ahead and landed high upon the castle's Keep. From there, she could see the whole castle, including the magnificent courtyard. It had once been a dusty open arena where wolves fought over scraps of putrefied meat. What she now saw took her breath away. The courtyard had been transformed into a wonderland of flowering trees. Within the massive courtyard, there were blue Chinese wisterias, pink velour myrtles, white snow weeping fountains, and, of course, soft purple jacaranda trees. There were apple trees, peach trees, and rows of juice-bursting, summer-crisp pear trees. She was excited to see delightful, succulent cherries and plump, luscious strawberries. There was everything a canary could ever dream of. This was an absolute fairyland for songbirds. Then she witnessed an absolute dreamscape created for otters. Cool pools of crystal-clear water with rocks and slides and everything that makes an otter's heart explode with joy. There were buckets and buckets of sea urchins, crabs, mussels, and clams to eat while floating on a warm sunny day. She couldn't wait until Paffuto and the rest of her friends saw what was waiting for them. *They can't even imagine what has been prepared for them*, she thought.

She was also amazed to see so many animals living together in one place. She witnessed hundreds of hamsters milling about and doing every task imaginable, from painting tool sheds to pruning lavender bushes. Splendid parrots of every kind were perched atop castle walls, showing off their magnificent colors. African grays, rainbow lorikeets, blue-throated macaws, lovebirds, and cockatiels chattered about everything and nothing. She saw ring-tailed cats chasing one another up and down the castle flagpole. There were bufflehead ducks quack-laughing and playing barnyard tag. There were chimpanzees playing conkers and red pandas feeding Silkie chickens. She saw finger monkeys riding on the backs of slithering green corn snakes. She even saw a kangaroo hopping up and down, high into the branches of a peach tree to gather tender, mouth-watering peaches. This was truly a magical place, and Cola couldn't wait to tell Paffuto what she had seen. She lifted her wings and flew back to the opera of canaries who had been waiting to hear news that would lift their spirits.

Still at the bottom of the steep hill, they all looked up to see that the castle was finally within reach without anyone to block their way. Before the final climb, the hamsters opened their rucksacks to share what they had with the canaries and otters. They would all need a hearty breakfast in order to make it up the steep hill. There were figs, seeds, pears, and even a wee loaf of dry bannock. They even shared a butterfish with the otters that they had just recently caught. It turned out that there was more than enough for everyone, and even a few leftovers. But the canaries loved the juicy pears the most.

"Sorry we haven't fresh clams for you," said Two-Spots to the otters. "But if I'm bein' honest and true, I'd rather be gobblin' a fresh brambleberry tart." As soon as he heard himself say *brambleberry tart*, he started looking far off and licking his lips, imagining how it would satisfy his sweet tooth and empty belly. He looked as if he was locked in a trance, lost in his enjoyment of an imaginary sugary tart.

"That tart sure has got a monkey grip on his imagination," observed Harry.

"He's off with the fairies," observed Melon, "and I'm not sure he's comin' back."

"We're sooo...sorry, Two-Spots," Corky said teasingly. "When we were preparing for battle with the dark wolf and rushing out of the castle to save our friends here, we must've forgot to pack your *brambleberry tart*. A thousand pardons."

"We are very grateful for everything you have so graciously shared with us," said Harry Otter to the hamster archers. Paffuto and all the canaries were ravenously attacking the seeds and figs. The canaries would never believe that Paffuto's head could get any bigger than it was, until they saw how many seeds and pears he crammed into his drippy gob. His cheeks swelled up like a puffer fish. All the canaries were enjoying the sweet, sloppy pears as their tiny bird tongues had never experienced such an eye-popping delicacy.

"This is just a small taste of what is to come," said Wendell with a hearty laugh. "The castle has many surprises waiting for all of you. They have been planning your arrival for a long, long time."

The canaries and the otters felt puffy and stuffed from snack-gobbling, but they were now ready for their final climb to the castle. Just as they set off to ascend the hill, a rustling in the brush along the path in front of them drew their attention. Out of the brush and briars stepped Rubacuori and Rodolpho, along with the other misled canaries. They were thin and gaunt, their feathers straggly. The hamster archers immediately drew their bow and needle arrows and pointed them at the bedraggled birds. Paffuto didn't recognize the birds at first but then recognized Rubacuori's blue feathers under a powdery layer of dust.

"Wait!" ordered Paffuto. "I know these canaries."

"Hello, Paffuto," said Rubacuori quietly, with his head down. He felt ashamed and couldn't look Paffuto in the eyes. Paffuto remained still, waiting to hear what Rubacuori had to say.

"I never should have followed him," Rubacuori admitted. "My pride drove me away from everyone that I love and everyone that loves me. I feel foolish for listening to him. He promised us everything, but we came away with nothing. I'm heartbroken for leading Rodolpho and the others away from you and their families. I didn't guard *my* own heart, so I wasn't able to help them guard *theirs*. My wings should be clipped! I'm not worthy to fly with you, Paffuto! I am so lost and ashamed and I…"

Paffuto didn't utter a word. He simply drew close to Rubacuori and wrapped him in his strong wings. Rubacuori burst into tears as he melted under the loving wings of the giant canary. Rodolpho drew close to Paffuto as well. Paffuto then opened his wings wider as the other tattered canaries drew close to seek their own forgiveness. No more words were spoken. There was simply a sweet understanding that *all* was forgiven, and the wayward canaries would still have a home in the castle. The thought of his selfish wanderings would come back to haunt Rubacuori from time to time. His mind would tell him that he wasn't worthy, but he knew that Paffuto had *chosen* to forget his muddles and missteps. Whenever Rubacuori was plagued with guilt about his own drifting heart, he would simply look into Paffuto's eyes, and forgiveness was found again. The miracle of *forgiveness* was then followed by a deep, satisfying *rest*.

The seven hamsters reached back and guided the arrows back into their quivers. The tiny rodent warriors felt humbled to lead Paffuto, the otters, and a magnificent parade of joyful canaries to the castle. To guide a new heart to the castle was the greatest of all honors. Paffuto now knew why they hadn't climbed the final hill yet. Rubacuori and his followers would have been left behind. Everything that he had gone through was worth it, in his mind, if it meant more canaries could enter the castle. A few of the canaries grumbled when Paffuto asked Rubacuori to join him in the front of the other canaries to fly toward the castle, but Paffuto was so overwhelmed with joy that the lost canary came back that he wanted to honor his humility and celebrate a canary that was found again.

So Paffuto flew ahead with Rubacuori and the other canaries as Wendell Cheeks and the other hamsters led the otters up the very steep hill along winding paths.

They finally arrived at the top the hill and approached the castle with unbridled joy and excitement. As they stood at the edge of the moat, their hearts stirred with emotion.

Some laughed, some cried, and some just stared up at the castle walls, hardly believing that they had finally arrived. They heard a sudden single blast of a trumpet; and Archimedes, the silverback gorilla who worked in the gatehouse, began turning the windlass. The thick, heavy chains began to creak and groan as the old wooden drawbridge descended. The ground shook as the bridge hit the ground on the other side of the moat. Paffuto and his followers caught a breathtaking glimpse inside the castle from across the moat. They stepped slowly on to the ancient wooden bridge. As they started to cross, their hearts began to beat faster as the glory of the castle came into full view.

Chapter 37

Coeur des Coeurs

Paffuto and his friends entered the castle courtyard with eyes opened wide and hearts opened even wider. They were overwhelmed as they moved slowly and silently into the courtyard. Everyone was speechless; only gasps could be heard as they tried to absorb all the beauty around them.

"As sure as eggs is eggs, we're in the wrong place," declared Water Kitty as she broke the silence. Everyone agreed. None of them felt they deserved what they saw before them. Even the fledglings in Melon's basket remained quiet and still, trying to take in all the castle's beauty.

This somber moment was suddenly interrupted as Barnaby Bunch and Captain Nibbles entered the courtyard through the open portcullis. They greeted Wendell Cheeks and the other hamster archers first.

"Well done, Wendell Cheeks!" shouted Barnaby. Then they greeted Chewy, Corky, Two-Spots, Toby, Lola, and Rosie, all faithful hamster servants of the castle. After praising them for their dedication and service, he looked up at Paffuto who towered over everyone in the castle. "And welcome, Paffuto, our honored guest. Your heroics have inspired us all."

"My, you are a very...large...bird," said Captain Nibbles, bending his neck back to look up at Paffuto. "We heard your thunderous chirp from inside our castle walls. Quite impressive, I must say. At first, we thought that Two-Spots missed his lunch, and his stomach was growling during the battle." Everyone laughed except Two-Spots. It just reminded him that he was quite ready for a hearty meal, and he still hadn't stopped dreaming about that brambleberry tart.

"You must be thirsty, my friends," said Barnaby. "Come and drink your fill from the Providence Spring! Be refreshed by the Eau de Vie!"

Harry and Kitty did not have to be asked twice. They were extremely parched from their journey. The two otters tripped and rolled over each other to get to the well. They were so excited that they forgot that Melon couldn't run with his painful wounded paw. The large otter hobbled on three paws as fast as he could, even though he was in extreme pain. Paffuto and the other canaries followed and surrounded the well. Two elder capuchin monkeys, who oversaw the well, drew buckets of the cool sparkling water and filled silver cups to the brim. They passed them around to outstretched hands. It was the sweetest and most satisfying water that had ever touched their lips. When Melon finally reached the well, one of the monkeys noticed his damaged paw. He also saw that Melon was wincing in severe pain.

"I think you will enjoy this water even more than the others," said the monkey to the limping otter. "Eau de Vie!" shouted the monkey. "Water of life! You will never want to drink from another well!" Melon graciously took the cup from the monkey and drank every drop of the sweet water. He felt a strange sensation run through his body. First, he felt a twinge, then a tickle, then a tingle all the way down to his paw bone. He immediately stood up on his hind legs and began to dance a most unrestrained jig. Everyone around him noticed that his crushed paw was better than ever! In an instant, Melon went from a painful limp to a giddy jig. Imagine that! From a limp to a jig! He had no more pain and certainly no more tears. Kitty laughed at her twin otter.

"I think from henceforth, you shall be called...Sir Jigalot," she declared to Melon, then rolled on the ground with laughter. Melon was a horrible and awkward dancer, but he didn't care a fig! This made Kitty laugh even harder. She had never seen her brother so enthusiastic. Harry desperately tried to control his laughter at the sight of his large jigging brother. He was slightly embarrassed because he didn't think it was proper to be so spirited and energetic in front of Barnaby and the captain. But when he saw that Melon's foot was healed, he understood why his brother was so joyful and carefree. So Harry gave in and laughed with his sister, Water Kitty. They all took paws and jigged in a circle together.

"Go, Sir Jigalot!" Harry yelled to Melon as the three of them spun in a circle. Otters *are never* ashamed of their joy, and they are *never* embarrassed to express themselves wholeheartedly. A healing of miraculous proportions always results in a flood of tears, uncontrollable laughter, and healthy doses of spirited jigging.

After drinking the water of life to their hearts' content, their hearts were opened even wider to see all the glory and splendor of the castle. Every sound they heard was like music, and every smell was like the aroma of springtime. There were new colors that they had never seen! Even the castle horses looked like they had been plunged in silver and gold. They shimmered in the sunlight, and they were breathtaking! These were the *horses of paradise* that they had been told about.

"Why do they shimmer in spectacular shades of silver and gold?" asked Water Kitty.

"They're simply gifts to enjoy. Look around you and see how Splendor abounds! Sometimes you give good gifts to your children just to bring them joy." Barnaby laughed.

"All the beauty you see has always been right here, waiting for you."

"It's butter on my bacon—that's what it is," added Melon as he stared at the radiant, gleaming horses.

"But we can hardly look at those horses or anything else in the castle. Everything takes our breath away and brings tears to our eyes," said Harry Otter.

"That's how you know you are home," answered Barnaby softly.

After the new arrivals were finished refreshing themselves at the Providence Spring, Sir Desmond Hillary Fitzhugh and his elite squadron of bomber pigeons spiraled slowly to the ground and landed in front of Barnaby and Captain Nibbles.

"Greetings, Sir Desmond!" shouted Barnaby Bunch. "Mission accomplished! You and your squadron have defended us once again. We are forever in your debt." Then Barnaby raised his voice so *all* could hear. "Men-at-arms and all domestic servants, Sir Desmond had informed me before this heroic mission that this would, indeed, be his last hurrah! He is retiring to a life of reflection and much-deserved leisure!" There was an echo of disappointed moans throughout the courtyard, followed by a slowly building chorus of applause and cheers. Sir Desmond stepped forward to address the crowd.

"Now, now, take courage, my friends. I have been in service to the castle my whole life, save my fledgling years. I'm an old, creaky sky bird now, and my flappers aren't what they used to be. It's time to hand off the old goggles and flight cap to my successor. You will always be my *coeur des coeurs*, my very heart of hearts." He slowly took off his goggles, then his aviator cap, and handed them to Captain Nibbles. He raised his wing and saluted Barnaby and the captain. The whole squadron of bombardiers saluted Sir Desmond Hillary Fitzhugh as they began to shout in unison,

> Hippity, pippity, hip hip hooray,
> Sir Desmond, you've earned your Fly-Away Day!
> Three cheers and a whoopee, a bravo, a yay,
> Hippity, pippity, hip hip hooray!
>
> The western sky greets you,
> You finished the race.
> Fly off toward the sunset
> With warmth on your face.
>
> Well done, faithful servant!
> You gave it your all,
> You opened your heart,
> You heeded the call.

> Hippity, pippity, hip hip hooray!
> One million cheers, a bravo, a yay,
> We salute you, Sir Desmond
> On your Fly-Away Day!

When they finished, all the bombardier pigeons threw their flight caps high in the air to celebrate their commander's retirement. Sir Desmond stepped forward as Captain Nibbles presented him with two distinguished medals. The first was the prestigious Birdman's Medal, only given to birds of character and valor. The next was the Aerial Achievement Medal, given to sky commanders who have demonstrated both courage and selflessness during aerial conflict. The heavy medals clanged against each other when they were placed around his neck. He looked down at them with humility as they rested on his chest. They were magnificent medals for a magnificent sky commander. Sir Desmond saluted, then turned and took his place with his fellow pilots as Captain Nibbles still held his leather aviator cap and flight goggles in his tiny hamster hands. Barnaby knowingly nodded to Captain Nibbles, and the captain cleared his throat before speaking.

"It is time to commission a new sky commander as Sir Desmond has now officially retired," declared Captain Nibbles. Everyone held their breath as they waited to find out who the new sky commander would be. Low mumblings and speculations could be heard throughout the courtyard. Then Captain Nibbles spoke after clearing his throat.

"Paffuto Serinus Canaria, please step forward," said Captain Nibbles in his most official yet squeaky hamster voice.

"That's you, Paffuto!" shouted Cola. She got behind him and tried to push him forward but couldn't budge the massive five-hundred-pound canary.

"Step forward, big canary!" yelled Harry Otter.

"Go ahead, Paffuto!" shouted Water Kitty.

"What are you waiting for?" asked the other canaries. Paffuto moved slowly and awkwardly toward Captain Nibbles and Barnaby Bunch. He inched his way forward and looked at them shyly.

"Paffuto, you *do not* have the flying skills of the fearless falcon. And you *do not* possess the vision of the mighty eagle. And you certainly *do not* boast the majestic wingspan of the magnificent Andean condor," began Captain Nibbles.

"He is *not* very good at handing out compliments," whispered Melon to Harry and Kitty.

"Shhh… He's leading up to something," said Harry.

Then Captain Nibbles continued, "But you have learned to overcome your…condition. You have saved countless lives. You have outwitted your enemy. And…most importantly, you have displayed a heart of compassion and sacrificed yourself for others and for the well-being of the castle. You are the biggest bird we have ever seen yet, through your humility, have made yourself smaller than any creature of the castle or the forest. You have decreased so others around you could increase. You are indeed a servant's servant! I proclaim, on this glorious day, that you, Paffuto Serinus Canaria, be elevated to the supreme position of sky commander!"

A loud cheer rose to the heavens. A delirious ovation erupted amid thunderous shouts and blaring trumpets. A celebration of approval echoed throughout the courtyard. One small canary stepped through the crowd with tears streaming down her face. It was Paffuto's mother, Edna. She openly wept with a mother's joy as she looked up at her baby boy. He was no longer being ridiculed, mocked, and humiliated. He was finally being respected, honored, and admired. Edna's heart was now full.

Barnaby and the captain stood looking up at Paffuto, still clutching Sir Desmond's aviator cap and his flight goggles. Their intention was to place them on Paffuto's head, but they realized that they would never be able to squeeze them on his massive feathered head.

"In due time we will have you fitted properly for your new uniform, Sky Commander Paffuto," said Barnaby. "For now, you can fly in your hatchday suit."

Hundreds of canaries then made a circle around Paffuto and offered him a new song that celebrated their new hero.

> Plumpy, lumpy, chubby, and brave
> His heart and soul, to us he gave.
> Tubby, blubby, pudgy, and good
> For truth and honor, he always stood.
>
> He led us through the darkest night,
> He went before us in our fight.
> In times of trouble, pain, and strife,
> He gladly gave his only life.
>
> Your soul, Paffuto, is brave and true,
> You gave your all to see us through.
> Tales of your courage will be told,
> Your heart, Paffuto, is made of gold.

"Paffuto Serinus Canaria, prepare *your* RBW to take flight." It was time to begin his life as the new sky commander. So he took a very deep breath, tilted his head back, and erupted with the *seventh chirp*. "CHIRP!"

The whole castle erupted in an explosion of cheers. Parrots squawked wildly. Monkeys chattered without restraint. Twin baby elephants used their trunks to trumpet their unbridled excitement. Even the spotted turtles tried to join in by opening their mouths to make the loudest sound a spotted turtle can possibly make. Sadly, no one could hear their turtle sounds, and most thought they were just yawning. The fledglings in Melon's basket joined in the celebration by flapping their wings with joyful exuberance. But this time, they did not remain in the basket. Their little bodies suddenly felt lighter, and they found themselves rising into the air. Cholena proudly flew above them. They imitated her every move and were soon flying next to her. The birdlings flew awkwardly, following Cholena high above the castle courtyard. Otter Melon looked up and watched them fluttering in the sky. He was so delighted that he began to hop, skip, and jig, now that his paw was fit as a fiddle. *His* tiny birdlings had made it safely home and were finally doing what gave them great joy. They had waited so long, and now they were flying! Just as the fledglings had finally found their wings, the eggs in Water Kitty's basket were cracking open at the same time. As they broke through their tiny blue shells, the tiny hatchlings chirped loudly for their parents to join them. Proud moms and dads flew down to celebrate the hatch-day of their little ones. It was a miraculous time of new life and fresh beginnings.

One birdling, named Dinkleman, was very excited and far too careless. This caused him to fly headfirst into the castle flagpole. The other birdlings, flying with Cholena, began to laugh and even started to make up a rhyme about the clumsy bird. "Don't be a Dinkleman, don't be a Dinkleman," they sang.

Cholena scolded them immediately by saying just two words. "Remember Paffuto!" she said sternly. "You might be a Dinkleman today, but someday soon, you could become the next Paffuto." Dinkleman's fellow birdlings felt ashamed, then flew back to make sure that he was not hurt. Unkindness was a poison and not permitted in the castle. If you teach birdlings to be kind when they first find their wings, they will probably grow up to be very kind and compassionate flyers.

The RBW waited for a signal from Paffuto. He began to flap his wings and lift his massive body into the air. As he lifted himself up into the bright cloudless sky, the squadron of royal pigeons followed. Thus began Paffuto's first patrol of the forest surrounding the castle. The Royal Bird Wing would continue to defend anyone who would heed the call of the castle. They would shelter anyone who would gather under the shadow of their wings. And they would lead them safely to the castle, where unimaginable wonders were waiting for them.

Cola sat perched on a very thin branch in a narrowleaf willow tree. Her heart was filled with overwhelming joy and deep pride as she watched Paffuto lift away with the Royal Bird Wing. She was the only one who believed in him from the beginning. Today, Paffuto's happiness was *her* happiness. He looked back and found Minuscola's smiling face. He smiled back. They didn't speak, but they both knew that he had to fly on. This was a magnificent day to fly up into a soft blue sky.

Epilogue

Deep in the forest, at the site of Serigala's attack, white statues of angry beasts stood hauntingly lifeless. Serigala stood motionless, baking in the warm midmorning sun. He was completely covered in a thick and heavy incrustation of pigeon droppings. Sanguinaire, the murderous bobcat, was now cold and lifeless. His face was a hideous frozen grimace. Sir Walter Fat Belly and his two gutless friends, Dingus and Butkus, were forever trapped in a dried whitewash of pigeon dung. They were not found close to the battle. They were pigeon blasted while fleeing into a deeper part of the forest. Their cowardly hearts were leading them away from the battle. Their cowardice would always be remembered as they would have frozen expressions of fear, forever fixed on their faces.

    A very large cinnamon bear, with rusty brown fur, slowly emerged from the thick trees on the edge of the former battlefield. He ambled around the site very slowly, stopping to sniff the ground, then stand on his hind legs to sniff the air around him. He walked sluggishly up to a statue and found himself nose-to-nose with the wolf king statue. The bear cocked his head sideways as he could hear the faintest of moans from underneath the white plaster that covered the great wolf. The wolf seemed to be crying out for someone to release him, for someone to crack the hardened shell that covered him from nose to tail. His whimpers begged someone to set him free.

    Just as the bear raised a large paw to crack the chalky prison that held Serigala, he heard the buzzing of flapping wings overhead. He grunted, turned his head, and looked up into the cloudless blue sky. Flying overhead was the RBW, being led by the biggest yellow canary he had ever seen. This was the great Paffuto that he had heard about. The cinnamon bear now had a great decision to make. He could release the wolf with one swift swipe of his strong paw, or he could ignore the wolf's begging and wander back into the dense forest, leaving him there forever. The bear paced back and forth in front of Serigala's hardened white statue. What to do? What…to…do?

Notes for Part 1 and Part 2

Captain Nathaniel Nibbles
Oldest and wisest of the sixty-two hamsters, Captain Nibbles is a natural leader. He shows a weakness of faith for not believing in the power of the stones at the waterfall, but soon his faith is strengthened when Wendell comes back to life. He was on his way to knighthood when "fateful circumstances" or "a series of poor decisions" changed the course of his life. Captain Nibbles is a brave soul who stands up to Ratafia, the castle rat, as well as Serigala, the wolf king.

Chadwick the Holy
The spiritual leader of the hamsters left in charge of the hamsters at Fort Chewy. Always ready to strengthen the hamsters who are weak of faith. Reads and applies the *Book of Light*, reminding the other hamsters that they are in need of a much higher power in order to survive and fulfill their destinies.

Chewy
A hamster with a multitude of skills, including the skillful use of his extra sharp and durable teeth. He also has remarkable marksmanship skills with a bow and arrow. His leadership skills make him a possible successor to Captain Nibbles.

Two-Spots
A white hamster with one brown spot around his left eye and a black spot around his right eye. He is a very well-fed hamster with two things on his mind most of the time: eating and sleeping. He is overweight, and it gets him in trouble when he stands before the wolf king. He is not hero material, but he is an exceptional archer.

Instead of saving a duckling from a waterfall, he gets slapped by a fish instead. He makes no apologies for his large belly hanging over his dagger belt or his loud sleeping habits.

Wendell Cheeks

A slight and tiny hamster who has issues with a severe lack of confidence. He wants to be noticed and wants to be useful; however, he feels invisible. Is it a lack of self-esteem, or is it pride? Captain Nibbles sees him and understands him, then tries to draw the hero out of him. Wendell experiences the power of the life stone. His name is Cheeks for a reason.

Tobias Von Schnee (Toby)

Another "royal" hamster by birth. Born into a noble Bavarian hamster clan. Also, an award-winning member of the Royal Bavarian Archery Brigade. He was kidnapped by an enemy of the Bavarian State. He escaped, and as he attempted to make his way home, he became hopelessly lost. But as providence would have it, he was found by Barnaby Bunch who lovingly took him back to the pet shop to be with other hamsters. He tried to tell them who he was, but they became indignant with what they thought was his air of superiority. They only called him Toby from that day on. An outstanding archer, Toby gains their respect with his amazing archery skills.

Lola and Rosie

Sisters who lived the perfect hamster life with their parents in the home of a young girl named Madeline. They had all the blessings that hamsters could possibly have. But one day tragedy struck, which would change their lives forever. The family also owned a cat named Margo. Let's just say that the hamster parents sacrificed their lives so that Lola and Rosie could live. When Madeline came home from school one day and discovered the horror, she no longer wanted anything to do with caring for hamsters, and her father dropped Lola and Rosie off at Stumpy's Pet Shop. Both sisters were blessed with amazing "tracking" skills. They are known to have incredible "sniffers" and were both highly regarded by Captain Nibbles. Lola is instrumental in helping the hamsters escape from the wild boars.

Nashoba

In the Choctaw Native American language, Nashoba means "wolf." Nashoba Tek means "she-wolf," and Nashobushi means "wolf cub." Nashoba is a subservient wolf, second-in-command to Serigala.

Serigala

Serigala is the Indonesian word for "wolf," from the Sanskrit word *srgala*, meaning "jackal." Serigala is a predatory animal, one of the top carnivores in the food chain. He is the wolf king who uses the dark arts to control all. He is one bad wolf!

The Oubliette

A secret dungeon with access only through a trapdoor in the floor of the regular dungeon. Once you are dropped through the trapdoor, your only escape is now on the ceiling. Also called a *bottle dungeon*. From the French, meaning "to forget." Because of this, it is thought that it is somewhere you were thrown and forgotten about until you died. Nicknamed the Ouboo.

Garderobes

The garderobe was simply a stone seat with a hole in it, hidden by a curtain. Think of a port-a-potty. Garderobes emptied down a shoot, from the Keep that led straight into the moat, or a pit called a cesspool. It was the job of a gong farmer to empty the latrine pit.

Portcullis

Part of the internal defense system of a castle. It was a heavy gate of wood with spikes protruding from the bottom that was winched up and down to let people in and out.

Murder Holes

Also called *meurtrieres*. They were holes in the roof above the gate passage, used to throw down heavy stones or hot oil on the enemy once they got inside the castle. Water could be poured through the murder holes to put out fires as well.

Arrow Loops

Inside the castle, defenders shot arrows through loops or slits in the stone walls. They were designed to give as wide a view of the outside as possible, while being too small for enemy missiles to get inside.

Keep

The main stone tower inside the castle walls. It housed the living quarters for the castle's residents. This is where Serigala slept and ate. This is where the hamsters and rats fought the wolves, an epic battle between good and evil.

Purifying Silver

A silversmith in the story, a badger, purifies the silver over an open flame. He skims the dross, or impurities, off the surface. The process is completed when the silversmith can see his own reflection in the melted silver (Malachi 3:3).

Providence Spring

At the end of the story, Captain Nibbles strikes the water stone on the ground and a freshwater spring opens in the earth. It provides everyone in the castle not only with fresh water, but with renewed hope and faith. This event mirrors a true story of God's providence during the Civil War at Andersonville Prison in Georgia. This Confederate prison housed Union soldiers in very harsh conditions. The prisoners had no clean drinking water. They prayed without ceasing. Lightning struck the ground in the living area of the prison. A freshwater spring opened up in the earth, and the prisoners were spared death due to dehydration. Today, a permanent memorial is built on the site where lightning struck, and a freshwater spring emerged.

THE LOST HAMSTERS OF BARNABY BUNCH

Name Translations
Paffuto: Chubby Serigala—Indonesian for "Wolf"
Minuscola: Tiny Morte—Death
Rubacuori: Heartbreaker Morendo—Dying
Sanguinaire: Bloodthirsty Alzati Sopra—Rise Above
Cholena: Delaware Indian for "Bird"

The Fledglings
  The fledglings' names honor characters from Charles Dickens's novels. You might remember Jack Dawkins, better known as the Artful Dodger from *Oliver Twist*, or Jingle from *The Pickwick Papers*. Tilly Slowboy from *The Cricket on the Hearth* is represented as two characters in Paffuto. Belle was Scrooge's former fiancée in *A Christmas Carol*, and Jasper was found in *The Mystery of Edwin Drood*. I've always had a fascination with Charles Dickens and his works. My great-great-grandfather worked for James Vick, the international seedsman, as his bookkeeper. Mr. Vick moved from England to Rochester, New York, where my grandfather lived. James Vick and Charles Dickens were childhood friends, born in the same English town of Landport. They remained friends for the rest of their lives. Oh, the stories James Vick probably shared with my grandfather about Mr. Dickens.

Paffuto Quotes Shakespeare
  "Boldness be my friend: Arm me audacity from head to foot!" From *Cymbeline* c.1611 (Iachimo, Act 1, Scene 6). Paffuto changes *head to foot* to *beak to tail feathers*.
  When Paffuto hears about what awaits him at the castle (pink plums, huckleberries, and especially bumbleberry tarts), he declares his desire to be bold in the face of danger. He compares his present trials to future rewards. When Paffuto borrows Shakespeare's words of "Arm me audacity," he is saying, "Give me an intrepid boldness to run this race and finish this course." The tribulations that we face now are nothing compared to what awaits us (2 Corinthians 4:17) (light affliction vs. eternal weight of glory).

Morte and Morendo

The sibling vulture spies, commissioned by Serigala to monitor Paffuto's location. Morte means *death* and Morendo means *dying* in Italian. The significance is that they are scavengers and only eat things that are freshly killed. Their mother named them to constantly remind them of their role in life. They would grow up to be servants of death and live only to please Serigala and themselves. They even placed Serigala above their desire to satisfy their own hungers and cravings.

Nest of Vipers

Inspired by the annual viewing of seventy thousand snakes slithering out of dens to mate each spring in Narcisse, Manitoba, Canada. The event draws thousands of tourists and locals each year. The area around Narcisse is so attractive to snakes for the same reason many farmers abandoned it decades ago: its thin topsoil sits on top of limestone that water has gradually eroded underground, creating a network of small caves that can be entered through sinkholes.

Cholena's First Flight

Cholena flying for the very first time represents the new believer, awkward and clumsy in many respects, but still a monumental threat to the nest of vipers and a danger to their advances. "The vipers below were sorely disappointed, and they slithered back into their dark hiding places, mumbling to themselves." This is the power that even a new follower of Christ possesses even though they may be unaware of the unseen world and the war that their enemy is waging. There is also the idea that once a new believer takes flight, everything is wonderful and carefree, when in reality, the true warfare begins for him or her.

Full Wolf Moon

The first full moon in January has often been referred to as the wolf moon for centuries. Its origin comes from Native Americans who often heard wolves howling during cold winter nights at this time of year. The moon appears full for about three days, long enough for Serigala to call to anyone who will follow him. Serigala's howling in the night represents a spiritual enemy who hopes to lure followers with haunting lies and dark deceptions. Some of Paffuto's followers listen to Serigala's howlings and are deceived to follow him. Later, they return to taste the goodness and forgiveness of the giant yellow canary.

Spend a Penny

Spend a penny means to go to the toilet. The expression is derived from the fact that public toilets were installed in the United Kingdom in the mid-1800s that required a penny to be unlocked.

The Glastonbury Thorn

The Glastonbury thorn is a common hawthorn found in and around Glastonbury, Somerset, England. The tree is also widely known as the holy thorn, a term referring to the original legendary tree. (Many grafts from the original tree have been planted in the Glastonbury area.) It is associated with legends about Joseph of Arimathea and the arrival of Christianity in Britain. A flowering sprig from the tree is sent to the British monarch every Christmas and placed on the royal dining table. According to legend, Joseph of Arimathea visited Glastonbury with the Holy Grail. He thrust his staff, which once belonged to Jesus, into Wearyall Hill. The staff flowered, then grew into the original thorn tree. In Paffuto, he and his friends find shelter in its branches and are physically and magically hidden by being made invisible, so Serigala and Sanguinaire are unaware of how close they are to them. The Glastonbury thorn makes the enemy blind and deaf to Paffuto's presence, keeping him and his entire company of otters and canaries safe.

Guns, Guns, Guns, and Pickle

Originally used by pilots to alert their wingmen that they are in dogfight range and firing their cannon as opposed to their longer-range missiles. "Guns, guns, guns" is a blunt fighter pilot way of saying, "You're dead!" And the nickname for a little red button that US military aviators push to drop a bomb is Pickle! Paffuto was fortunate enough to have an experienced RBW to help him against the evil Serigala and his army. Sir Desmond deserved all the praise and honor that he received! He's one bad pigeon!

Chapter 18—Psalm 63:7

The Seventh Chirp

Seven was symbolic in ancient Israelite culture and literature. It communicated a sense of "fullness" or "completeness." It also related to divine perfection. The first use of the number 7 in the Bible relates to the creation week in Genesis 1. Also:

- Seven colors in the rainbow, a sign of God's promise to Noah.
- Command for animals to be at least seven days old before being used for sacrifice (Exodus 22:30).
- The command for leprous Naaman to bathe in the Jordan River seven times to be cleansed (2 Kings 5:10).
- The command for Joshua to march around Jericho for seven days (and on the seventh day to make seven circuits) and for seven priests to blow seven trumpets outside the city walls (Joshua 6:3–4).
- Additional examples: Gen. 7:2, Exod. 25:37, Isa. 11:2, Prov. 6:16, Matt. 18:22, Rev. 1:4, Rev. 1:12, Rev. 1:16, Rev. 5:1, Rev. 8:2. In all, the number 7 is used in the Bible more than seven hundred times. Paffuto's seventh chirp indicates perfect peace and completion.
- Seven hamster archers. Mother canaries sat on the eggs two weeks (2x7). Cholena was the seventh nestling to climb aboard Paffuto's back for her ride down to the basket.

Akhal-Teke

The Akhal-Teke is a Turkmen horse breed. They have a reputation for speed, endurance, intelligence, and a distinctive metallic sheen. The shiny coat of the breed led to their nickname, Golden Horses. They are magnificent horses that shine in the sun. There are considered to be the rarest horse breed on earth with less than seven thousand in existence. They are also called horses from paradise.

Story Theme

Inspired by the true story of General Vinegar Joe Stilwell who, during WWII, led four hundred soldiers, nurses, and civilians through the jungles to safety in India. They fled from the approaching Japanese enemy who were sometimes only hundreds of yards behind them. They had to continually outrun and outwit their pursuers. Many of the people in Stilwell's group were weak and sick. Some didn't have shoes to protect their feet. He was able to lead them all to safety in horrific conditions. Likewise, Paffuto and Harry Otter lead hundreds of vulnerable canaries, fledglings, and even eggs through a forest toward a castle that was secured by characters in a previous story. While leading the songbirds toward the castle, they are being pursued by vicious predators. Just like Stilwell, they must outrun and outwit their pursuers.

Comparison of two events: Cola watching how Paffuto flew away (a changed life)

Away he went with hot tears splashing down his cheeks. Cola's heart was crushed as she watched her forever friend slowly flutter away (chapter 20, Before the Castle).

She watched Paffuto lift away with the Royal Bird Wing as her heart burst with pride. She was the only one who believed in him from the beginning (chapter 37, After the Castle).

About the Author

Michael Jude Schauer has enjoyed a deeply fulfilling career as a third-grade teacher. In retirement, he enjoys writing and spending time with his wife, four children, and eight grandchildren. His students have been his inspiration and the fountain of joy and creativity that he has drawn from over many years. His literary influences vary, from Charles Dickens and C. S. Lewis to George MacDonald and A. A. Milne. He was mesmerized by his grandfather's ability to weave a fantastical tale and his father's insatiable hunger for the written word. Michael's love of storytelling was a centerpiece in his classroom for many years, and he has always delighted in discovering the right word for the right situation, or as Mark Twain once said, "The difference between the right word and the almost right word is really a large matter—it is the difference between the lightning and the lightning bug." He also has a strong affinity for the parables that Jesus taught in the New Testament. This is reflected in his stories, as he uses symbolism, allegory, and apologues to convey deeper truths. Hopefully the reader will be drawn to heed the call of the castle and flee the howling wolf.

Printed in the USA
CPSIA information can be obtained
at www.ICGtesting.com
LVHW041959150924
790969LV00001B/77

9 798890 431165